TRANSIENT HEARTS

By

ZEE MONODEE

ა

Decadent Publishing Company
www.decadentpublishing.com

This book is a work of fiction. Names, characters, places, and incidents are the products of the author's imagination or used fictitiously. Any resemblance to actual events, locales or persons, living or dead, is entirely coincidental.

Published by Decadent Publishing Company, LLC

Look for us online at:
www.decadentpublishing.com

Printed in the United States of America

~DEDICATION~

To my writing posse: Natalie, Rae, Jessica, Vanessa, & Lynn. You gals keep me grounded. And a huge thank you to Sheri Fredricks, who helped with the horse-riding scenes—any and all mistakes in those are mine alone!

Chapter One

"You burn *water*?"

Shayne Morea tore her gaze from the blackened kettle on the stovetop to glare at Aurelie Parks, who sat at the pine table with her dark head bent over the cell phone in her hands. Probably updating her Twitter feed again. *Blast her.*

Aurelie glanced up, graphite-colored eyes growing wide, before she shook her head, sending her long dark tresses flying.

Flying hair has no place in a kitchen. Shayne bit back the reprimand. They were in the Heart's Anchor ranch's kitchen, not a professional one with stringent hygiene regulations. Certainly not *her* restaurant kitchen.

Aurelie scrunched her lips into a pout. "I had no clue how long the water would take to boil."

"Are you serious?"

When Aurelie shrugged and returned her attention to the phone, thumbs working overtime, Shayne threw her hands up and reached for a quilted potholder. The acrid smell of scorched metal and the stench of burning gas filled her nostrils, and she pinched the bridge of her nose to prevent a sneeze.

One does not sneeze in a kitchen, at least not without wearing a surgical mask.

Using a firm grip, she grabbed the kettle's handle and

brought the darkened pot to the sink. Water hissed off in a cloud of billowing steam when she opened the tap onto the unsuspecting victim of Aurelie's domestic incompetence. The sink's gleaming metal dimmed to a dull gray under the soot.

The compulsion to scrape and clean the whole space spick-and-span, brought on by years of her mother's nagging how the true worth of a woman showed in how well she kept her house, and her teachers' eagle-eyed inspections in the culinary-institute kitchens, sparked off like a gnawing in the back of her mind. The feeling grew and snowballed until she could focus on nothing except the stain resembling a raven's wing on the polished steel.

Shayne shut her eyes, forced herself to blank her mind, but she couldn't, thanks to the gritty pain. Closing her eyelids on the dried-out eyeballs chafed worse than a badly done microdermabrasion job. Bloody desert weather with its dry air and even drier environment. Wouldn't there be some restriction on the use of water to clean the sink, because to her British eye used to rain, mist, and rolling green countryside, the whole state of Wyoming seemed on the brink of the harshest drought ever.

And she had bigger fish to fry, in scalding oil.

She opened her eyes and glared at Aurelie. The girl tried to appear engrossed in her phone activity, but Shayne could swear a deep blush of shame crept up Aurelie's mocha-brown skin and perfect cheekbones.

The git. Aurelie had so conned her.

"When you asked me to come to Freewill, you said you'd help me."

Aurelie jumped up and slid the phone into the pocket of her jeans. "And I will!"

"How? By burning the kitchen down? I cannot believe it. You said you knew how to cook, and you had no problem making the *ras malai* dish after I sent you the recipe. You even e-mailed me a picture of how the dessert came out."

"I, uhm, might have stretched the truth a little there," the girl confessed with a sheepish grin.

Shayne blinked again. The more she did so, the more her eyes hurt, and the more her annoyance threshold threatened to give up. To hell in a hand basket; that's where she headed.

"What about the picture then?"

"I might've Photoshoped an image I found online."

Aurelie's *ras malai had* borne a striking resemblance to the green-pistachio-decorated depiction of thick milk cream and puffy, floating milk curd clouds on the *Haldiram* sweets boxes.

"Okay. Let me get this straight. You're not a cook?"

Aurelie shook her head.

"So why were you searching for a *ras malai* recipe on a Facebook group dedicated to Indian chefs?"

"Because I knew you guys would have the recipe, duh." Aurelie plopped her petite form down on her vacated chair.

"Yeah, but you get your kicks out of looking for recipes, when you don't cook?"

"I'm not the one who needed the recipe. Mrs. Harvey did."

Right. Did the road to hell induce a mind-wiping migraine? This promised to be a fabulous trip. Not.

"Mrs. Harvey," Shayne said. "Mrs. Evelyn Harvey; the same woman I'm supposed to teach how to make Indian sweets." She paused. "With *your hands-on help.*"

"Someone's got to handle the camera when we shoot how the dishes are made. We're supposed to make a video blog of the whole process, too, remember?"

The videos. Not only would she have to cook, alone, and with no sous-chef or even a kitchen aide, but she'd also be on film. She appeared unpresentable on most days, as her mother and aunts pointed out with their scathing tongues at every occasion, but in the desert weather.... *Bugger.*

The line on her cheek, from her nose to one corner of her mouth, itched. Shayne reached up and scratched, then remembered to make her fingers curl. She'd just pick at her skin and end up with a rash rivaling the nail gouges she'd made to her legs and arms anytime a tropical mosquito bit her; those bloodsucking insects had loved her thin British skin back when she had visited the island of Mauritius, where her parents came from. She did not need red streaks on her face, to add to the lizard-hide patches of dry skin on her cheeks, arms, and legs, on her arse, too, why not.

Bloody arid Wyoming climate. She never thought she'd miss the humidity of England, but right then, homesickness for the damp weather assailed her.

And she'd only been here for a day.

"How did I let you rope me into this mad scheme?"

"Ha! You're one to talk," Aurelie threw out. "Remind me again who cried out to me, desperate to escape her mother's clutches?"

Shayne groaned.

"Exactly." Aurelie gloated. "Who did she try hooking you up with? A hick from Bradistan who still cowered under the *palau* of his mother's sari?"

The glasses-wearing, stick-thin accountant from the Indians-filled town of Bradford, and the latest in the exhibit of "eligible" young men her mother and aunts had paraded in front of her, with increased speed and amplified desperation, ever since she'd turned twenty-seven the year before. The age of shame, when a modern Indian girl went on the shelf with dwindling matrimonial prospects in her future.

Shayne shivered at the memory. "Don't remind me of him."

"Okay. What about the industrialist from India who stated his wife would have to give him a male heir exactly nine months after their wedding night, or else he'd divorce her and go looking for another, more fertile uterus?"

Shayne groaned again, louder, and let her body drop onto a chair.

"Or, the rich merchant from Luckhnow who, despite not being a Muslim, wanted his wife to remain behind the modest screen of *purda* and not come into any contact with a male who is not him?"

Shayne let her head fall until her forehead hit the polished pine of the table.

"We're in May, and these are the prospects from March and April. Want me to go back? Let's see. Who else did the aunts include?"

She sat up straight and narrowed her eyes on her friend. Why on earth had she told Aurelie all of this? Shayne winced. Over the past two years, she'd come to rely on the e-mails she exchanged with her Facebook buddy as a lifeline to sanity.

"Okay, I get it," she said. "Being here is the lesser evil, right?"

"Exactly! You wanted your mom off your back, and you did it."

At what cost? She hadn't thought things through. When offered the prospect to escape from her parents in Southall, and the gaggle of matchmaking aunts in London, she'd jumped on the occasion. With these women, a girl had to live life by the moment, because no clue pointed to what madness they might spring at any given time. Shayne had grown tired of such a hectic existence, and the summer in Freewill had seemed like deliverance...into Purgatory. She still couldn't wrap her head around the idea that Aurelie couldn't even boil water.

On her own. Such became her fate here.

Snap out of the Bollywood melodrama, girl!

The itch on her cheek spread out to the back of her neck. The weight of her superthick, Indian hair—extra-dry, coarse, and with enough static electricity to power her laptop, thanks to the low humidity—rubbed the same as Brillo pads against the prickly skin.

At least there, the rash wouldn't be visible. Shayne gave in and scratched, until the telltale burn of broken skin told her she'd peeled off the sensitive thin barrier. When she pulled her hand back, smears of blood dappled under the short nails.

"Bloody hell, Aurelie. What the fuck am I doing here? This place is gonna drive me bat-shit crazy!"

"Crazier than your mother? I doubt it."

"Oh, bugger off, you sodding cow!"

"Why don't you buck up, bitch?"

The creak of the screen door resounded in the kitchen, but Shayne didn't care. Tears prickled at her eyes, and she snorted; she wouldn't need to use saline drops to moisten her dry eyeballs. She'd conjured the moisture up on her own. Not even cutting onions would call to tears here.

This place is Hell.

Whoever had been coming in must've retreated, because the door creaked again, probably closing on the person's departing figure.

"Oh. My. God!" Aurelie jumped to her feet and dashed to the door. "Grayson, wait!"

Shayne kept her head lowered and forced herself to breathe in and out, slow and deliberate inhales, so she could ward off the breakdown menacing to engulf her in its tsunami-like wave.

"I cannot believe it's you," Aurelie exclaimed.

A male grunt, like someone having the air punched out of them, greeted the exuberant words, and intrigued by the sound, she peeked up. Aurelie squeezed the life out of a tall, dark-haired man in an ink-blue suit.

"When did you get here?" the girl asked when she released him.

"Just now," he replied.

Aurelie took a step back and dragged him into the kitchen, her hand on his sleeve in what resembled a death grip. The rich fabric would crease. What a shame, when the suit screamed "tailor-made designer wear."

"Is this a bad time?" he asked.

With him in the room, Shayne heard him properly for the first time. His voice thrummed low, smooth, a soft drawl in the words.

The back of her neck prickled again, but from something else. Physical awareness. She squinted in his direction, careful to conceal she assessed him.

He wore a well-cut suit hugging a lean yet broad physique and Italian loafers on medium-sized feet. His big hands had well-cared-for nails. Above the collar of his crisp, light blue shirt, pale gold skin stretched on a chiseled jaw, and a thin-lipped mouth curled into a smile as he gazed at Aurelie. Shayne continued her perusal despite catching her breath at his smile. His nose appeared neither too sharp nor too soft, and a shock of unruly dark hair with wavy locks breaking from the swept-back style, brushed his wide forehead. But the eyes.... they proved the most beautiful eyes Shayne had ever seen on a man. They slanted upward at the outer corners, giving him an exotic look hinting at Asian blood, and the irises were dark—brown or black, she wondered?—framed by thick lashes and topped by heavy, dark eyebrows.

She gulped. Character radiated off his face, and his soft tone—such a man wouldn't need to raise his voice to be heard, or to make others listen. No, he had a quiet, subtle, and deadly edge that pulsated off his big, well-attired body.

Drat. Why did she have to meet such a devastating specimen when all dried-up, red, scaly, and with broken skin and blood under her nails?

Life worked against her lately.

As if you'd do anything if he glanced your way.

A tryst. What would be wrong with it? She didn't do permanent, not with her crazy family, where every male over forty and every female in her entourage wanted to see her "settled and secure."

"Married and tied-down to ideals, mores, and traditional roles," as she saw it. Not for her. Shayne had a life to live, a career to roll out, places to see. The right man hadn't come along thus far, and she wouldn't go searching for him, either. Better to be alone than unhappy, as she repeated every time the pang of loneliness clattered in her heart. Usually, under such circumstances, she'd go out looking for a bloke, a friend with benefits. No ripple to shatter the surface of her life's pond. She'd surrounded herself with male friends who would never disrupt the status quo, men who didn't do permanent.

And if she read the bloke here right, he also didn't do

permanent. Too aloof, composed, sophisticated. What was he doing here? No ring on the third finger of his left hand. Not married. Taken, maybe? Or commitment phobic, like most guys?

The two in front of her broke their hug, which tore Shayne out of her thoughts.

He brought Aurelie at arm's length. "You sure have grown."

"But you look just the same."

"Eighteen and gangly?"

"You filled out nicely, but your face." Aurelie's features clouded over as she brought a hand up and touched the man's cheek. "You've been away for too long," she said softly.

Uh-oh. Did she hear repressed feelings in those words? This bloke—a former love of Aurelie, maybe? In that case, he'd be off limits for her.

Provided he'd even be around for more than a day.

He nodded toward Shayne. "Won't you introduce us?"

Aurelie shook her head and pulled his hand, drew him closer to the table. "Silly of me. Grayson, this is Shayne, a good friend of mine. She just got here from England, and she's staying over for the summer—"

"She's staying here?"

Shayne bristled, spine growing tense, at the note of incredulity in his tone. *Excuse me?*

"Well, of course she is, silly."

"I thought," he started, looked away from Shayne, "it'd be just us. My mistake—"

The gall of him. Shayne jumped to her feet. "You know, if this is a private matter, I'll leave. There's got to be a place in town—"

"Don't be absurd," Aurelie said. "You're staying with us, period."

The man named Grayson, whom Shayne saw more as the "arrogant, stuck-up pig named Grayson," lowered his gaze farther and started at the door.

"I think this is a bad idea," he said.

"Don't be daft." Aurelie tugged on his arm. "You've come back home after fourteen years. You're not gonna leave already."

"I made a mistake—"

He stopped when the screen door burst open. His whole demeanor changed when his gaze landed on Tracy Parks, Aurelie's mother. He tensed his jaw, curled his hands into fists. If she squinted, she'd say for certain the set line of his pursed mouth trembled a little when the older woman stopped dead in her tracks and stared at him.

"Grayson," Tracy finally said in a whimper full of pain and longing.

"Aunt Tracy." His voice sounded even lower.

Tears trailed down Tracy's pale cheeks, and without another word, she reached out and enclosed him in her arms.

He stiffened, before he brought his arms up and clung to her frail body. He reminded Shayne of a lost child right then, and she frowned.

Aurelie had tears on her dark cheeks.

Family reunion. Totally awkward time for her. She took a step toward the hallway when Tracy broke the silence, exclaiming how happy Grayson had made her, and Shayne froze.

Blast. She came from Indian bloodlines, and she loved a good drama-filled moment. After all, she'd grown up on Bollywood fare and *Star One* and *Zee TV* soaps. Try as she wanted, she couldn't tear her feet from the floor to leave the room and give the Parks the privacy they deserved as they reunited with the Grayson fellow.

Who could this man be?

Curiosity ate at her, and she shifted from foot to foot, hoping Tracy would let her out of her inquisitive misery soon.

"I didn't dare hope you'd come back," Tracy said as she broke away from his embrace and peered up into his face, her voice coming out strangled, as if she battled sobs.

He chuckled, the sound devoid of humor. "You told me the

time had come to return."

"I tell you the same thing at every phone call."

But you never listen.

Even she could hear the unspoken words, and Grayson bowed his head. With shame, maybe?

"But never mind. You're here now; that's what matters." Tracy cupped his cheek. "You know you can stay for as long as you want. It is your home, after all."

"I better go get my things from the car." He shuffled his feet once or twice, and then tore out of the screen door and onto the porch. Through the window, Shayne and the other two women watched him fly down the steps to rush into the dark green Mercedes parked in front of the closed garage door.

Tracy wiped her tear-streaked cheek as she gazed out. "He's here," she said in a soft tone filled with awe.

"Uhm, who is he?" Shayne asked.

"Aurelie hasn't introduced you?"

"We didn't have time for introductions. Things sort of went downhill the minute he heard I would be living here. And speaking of, maybe I better move out, if he'll be staying—"

"Nonsense!" Tracy brushed her words away with a wave of her hand. "You're our guest. Grayson's been raised properly. He'll never retract the family's hospitality. This might be his ranch, but you're our guest. Period."

His ranch? Wait a minute....

He sat in the car, and through the tinted windows, she couldn't see what he was up to.

Aurelie yelped and grabbed Shayne's wrist in the same death grip she'd held Grayson's sleeve a few moments earlier. "We should've been at the Hometown Bakery fifteen minutes ago."

Great. Their first meeting with the woman who had been generous enough, or maybe crazy enough, to go along with their video blog and Indian sweets' recipes scheme, and they were late. What a brilliant first impression they'd make.

"Shayne, what's on your hands? Blood?" Tracy asked.

"I'll go wash up." She didn't want to get into an explanation with Tracy. Doing so would force her to think back on the dire climatic conditions in the area, which in turn would trigger her homesickness and wake up her foul mood. "And, Auntie, sorry for the kettle and the dirty sink."

Tracy laughed. "My daughter's been through the kitchen. Don't worry; I'll handle everything."

Aurelie grabbed Shayne's T-shirt sleeve to pull her through the corridor toward the front door. "We don't have time to allow for you to scrub your hands and forearms for fifteen minutes straight."

"I'll be cooking food for the woman, for God's sake. Don't you think such a position warrants clean hands?"

"Clean, yes. But you're not out to do brain surgery, so skip the antibacterial scrub brush."

"Oh, get lost, will you?"

"Girls!" Tracy warned from the kitchen.

The way Tracy dealt with their bickering, one would think she'd had a brood of children and had mastered the perfect tonal inflection to get them back in the ranks. No one would believe Shayne hadn't spent more than twenty-four hours under their roof. But then, Tracy used to work as an elementary-school teacher in California prior to coming to Wyoming. No wonder she could deal with squabbling brats.

Chastised, both girls trudged the rest of the way to the house's front, where Aurelie had parked her car. Shayne ducked into the powder room at the back of the main staircase and proceeded to scrub her hands clean as quickly as possible. When Aurelie thumped on the closed door, she grabbed a handful of tissues and dried her hands before pressing the door handle down with her elbow and pushing the panel open with a hip.

"Aren't you laying the whole clean-freak thing on a little too thick?"

"I'm a chef. Would any client trust me if I got germs and bacteria all over their food?"

"Eww, that's gross!"

"Exactly."

They stopped near the car. Aurelie peered up with a worried glance. "You want to drive?"

"Hello? On the wrong side of the road? It's a miracle I didn't get killed on my way here. Thank goodness the rental company sent someone to pick up the car. I am so not driving in your crazy country."

"It's not the wrong side of the road. And we'd get into town so much quicker if we could cut through the fields on horseback."

Shayne shivered. True, she had come to cowboy country here in Wyoming, but who would've thought this place still existed as Wild Wild Mid-West, where people preferred to go everywhere on horseback?

"We're late and it's your fault, because you burned the kettle."

They settled into the car, Aurelie behind the wheel. She set the car in gear and tore out of the driveway in a dust-heavy U-turn, all while talking to Shayne.

"No, it's not. We would've been gone already had Grayson not come in. I couldn't simply dump the cousin no one has seen in fourteen years on the doorstep and leave, could I?"

"Your cousin?"

"Grayson Warner. He's five years older than me and some hotshot stockbroker or something, works on Wall Street. Rich as Croesus. The ranch is his, in truth. Mom only took over when he left, after his parents' death. He hasn't been back ever since."

"And why has he returned now?"

"I have no clue. But I guess we'll find out."

He'd be staying, and in the same house as she. Actually, she lived here as a guest in his house, not Aurelie's. No wonder he'd been peeved when he heard she'd be there.

"Listen, if it won't sit well with him that I'm there, I better move into town. I'd also be closer to the bakery."

"Oh, shut up, Shayne. Listen to yourself. Grayson's not a

monster."

No. He's just an arrogant, rich, pompous arse.

And she'd be living with him.

Add the fact that Shayne remained stuck in Freewill—her other option being to go back home to the matchmaking front rooms of her aunts—with a domestically incompetent Aurelie, on her way to meet a sweet, old lady who would probably have no clue what *dhal* or *sooji* meant....

Lord, have mercy!

෦ଃ

He couldn't remain hiding in the car. Grayson knew that, but the memo refused to travel to his legs.

As he stared out the windshield, his sight blurred, merging the picture of the gleaming, whitewashed wood house with the shabby, peeling-paint dwelling he remembered from his youth. On the other side of the structure, hidden from view when one came onto the ranch, stood the original, sprawling one-story ranch house erected back in the mid-eighteen hundreds, when his ancestor had acquired the property, a little more than ten thousand acres of deeded land. The ranch had since then passed down through five more generations of Warners.

Today, the ranch belonged to him, but Heart's Anchor, as his mother had renamed the place, did not feel like home. The place where he grew up, yes, but not home.

So what the hell was he doing here?

Grayson let his forehead rest against the smooth leather of the steering wheel. He should've been in his Upper East Side penthouse, savoring a martini after the superb coup he'd pulled for a client two days ago on the Forex market. *Warner, Elliott, & Gallas*, his investment management firm, had been tagged with the reputation of having the Midas touch. In the past year alone, Grayson had made millions for a good many of the clients in his very exclusive portfolio. The commissions on those dealings had made him an even richer man, and the media touted him as one of the most sought-after bachelors in New York society. A reporter had dubbed him the real-life Chuck Bass. Whatever that meant, Grayson had thought at first, to find out later when he went digging folks likened him to a fictional rich young heir who played hard and partied harder.

Not so far from his reality. He did drink too much, party too hard, sleep even less, and play more intensely on the currency market.

He became the golden boy of New York, but at what cost?

Grayson played the FX market with an edge that had made his reputation as the most competitive shark in New York for the past ten years and said edge came with its price. Something ate at his soul, forced him to seek more satisfaction, more instant gratification each time. But the high never lasted, and so he reached across through his job like a gambler out to reap the best return.

Lately, even the best proved not enough....

Jay's visit had sealed his fate. His best friend and business partner, Jay Elliott, had stood in his living room and out-and-out confronted him over his reckless dealings.

"How much longer can you keep doing this?" Jay asked.

"Doing what?" Grayson played possum.

"The last-minute dealings, swooping in on the market in the nick of time to buy or sell currency. Not sleeping. You look like a zombie behind the façade you show the world."

"Shut up, Jay."

"I've remained silent for the past nine months. This started back in August—"

Jay wouldn't go there, would he?

"—around the same time as the anniversary of your parents' death. It's hit you bad this time."

"Fuck off!"

"I'm serious, Grayson. If you don't put a stop to it all, I will."

"How?"

"I'll contact every financial regulatory authority if I have to. The Financial Industry Regulation Authority, the US Securities and Exchanges Commission, the Commodities and Futures Trading Commission. Every one of them will know how far you're going in your little games on the market."

"You'll bring the lid down on our whole firm if you do this."

"If I have to, if it's the only way to make you see sense, then I won't hesitate, Gray. I mean it. You have to get yourself back on track."

He'd bristled, but his friend would act on the threat. Jay never issued any threat. For him to go there meant a whole lot of shit had hit the fan. "And what do you suggest I do?"

"Go back home. It's time you faced that place, those memories again."

Jay is spot-on. Grayson had been loath to admit it.

But his friend spoke the truth. He'd become a shadow of himself, always searching for something. *More what?* Not that he had a clue. This would lead him down a spiral of perdition.

Exactly like his father.

Staring from his penthouse's terrace as twilight's cloak fell on Central Park after Jay left, the realization had jolted him out of his apathy.

He would not take the same path as his father, the arrogant, selfish, self-centered bastard. If he faced the truth, he'd been all of that, too. He'd run away from Freewill to Harvard right after his parents' death, telling himself and everyone else he had to do this, but he could've come back, done more than give his aunt a power of attorney to handle all the ranch business in his absence. He didn't wish to face this place again after the funeral, so he'd run.

But a man could never run far enough, and the past always caught up with him.

Fourteen years since the old man died, moved out of his life, yet, his shadow still darkened Grayson's existence, polluted every waking moment, crept through his subconscious when he slept. Lately, he couldn't shut his eyes for more than an hour at a time, and lack of sleep spelled the ring of doom for anyone who needed a clear head and sharp instincts.

Enough is enough. To put an end to the creeping darkness, he had to come back, to face his past, and put it all behind him. Accept the fact that he was Bobby Warner's son, the Freewill Warners' blood flowing in his veins. Jay had also left him no other choice.

So here he ended up, back in Freewill, and cowering inside his rental luxury sedan.

Grayson snorted. A man didn't get anything done without taking steps forward, without taking risks.

He unlocked the doors, throwing them and stepping out. The May sun tickled his back, the heat through the linen and wool blend of his suit akin to a gentle caress. The rays would burn in a few minutes, though.

From the trunk, he pulled out his traveling case and his laptop bag, which he swung onto one shoulder. Securing the car with the press of a button on his key fob, he trudged toward the house.

Up the six plank steps he went, and onto the wraparound porch. His mother had wanted a dream country house with clapboard sidings and a porch all around the first floor. His father, who adored her, had obliged, and masked the original ranch into the new, sprawling dwelling. Bobby Warner had never thought he'd inherit the family land. Neither the heir nor the spare, the resident of a hippie community in New Jersey found himself the only Freewill Warner left when his two elder brothers died in a boating accident. Together with his wife, Patsy, they made do with the situation, and accommodated their carefree and easygoing lifestyle on the ranch, where their only child came into the world.

Grayson paused on the porch when his gaze landed on the swing in the far corner. His mother's favorite place. He didn't have to close his eyes to picture her, to go back to that one perfect, special moment with her.

Rain had been falling in sheets for hours since the morning; his mother sat watching the downpour from the swing. A nine-year-old Grayson played at her feet with his

Matchbox *cars. He'd been small and skinny, and his mother had no trouble pulling him up into her lap.*

He squirmed under the touch, which made her laugh. She tucked him in the crook of her arm and pressed her cheek to his hair.

"After the rain, there is always a rainbow, Grayson," she said. "A beautiful, sparkling rainbow. And one day, under the arc of those brilliant colors, you will find your very own princess."

"Girls are gross."

His mother laughed, the light, tinkling sound he remembered from when he was smaller, but which had stopped coming lately.

"So you say now, honey. But one day you won't think that way, one day when you'll no longer be my little boy."

Sadness tinged her voice, and Grayson had been at a loss how to comfort her. So he burrowed into her embrace, knowing she'd relish the gesture of affection, and together, they watched the rain fall.

He snapped out of the memory, and tore his gaze from the faded red roses on the swing's cushions. Taking two steps to the screen door, he pulled it open and stepped into the kitchen.

His aunt turned to him and smiled, coming up to him. She placed a small hand on his shoulder and squeezed.

"Everything okay, son?"

"Yes." *Mom.*

Grayson bit his tongue before the word came out. Gentle and golden-haired Tracy reminded him of his mother. If she had lived, she would've looked exactly like Tracy, her identical twin.

But his mother was gone, taken from him and everyone else because of his father's selfishness, because Bobby Warner had never grown up.

"Your room is ready," his aunt said. "I've kept it just the way you left everything, hoping every day you'd come back."

I don't want to be here, he wanted to say, but he couldn't.

Not to her.

"You'll have to share the bathroom with Shayne, though. Did Aurelie tell you she is staying with us?"

Shayne, right. The beautiful, dark-haired girl in the kitchen earlier. Also the one with the snobbish, BBC-anchor British accent and a potty mouth like a disciple of Gordon Ramsay. "She's a friend of Aurelie?"

"Yes. She just arrived from England."

Not a surprise really, for his cousin amounted to one heck of a character; her friend and she were bound to be two peas in the same pod.

"How long will she be here?"

"A few months. Why? Is there a problem?"

A cool edge seeped into her voice, the same tone she'd used in the past, when she'd had to take over here and work order back in the chaos his parents had wrought on their combined existence.

"None at all," he bit out through gritted teeth, more because he felt chastised like the teenager he'd been back in the day than because Shayne's presence hurdled his plans.

A beautiful woman under his roof. She might prove to be a good distraction, help him drudge through his imposed two weeks of exile. He wouldn't hurt her, of course; he wasn't that much of an ass. But maybe she could help him to make the time pass.

That's it. He'd get to know her. If more developed, great. If not, no problem.

"Listen," he started, "is it possible for me to settle in the studio above the garage?"

"Why would you want to go there?" Her face softened. "Too much, too fast. Right, son?"

"Yeah."

Grayson didn't hesitate to show her the true depths of his feelings, the swirling abyss inside him. Tracy knew him better than anyone else; he allowed her to see him for who he was inside, ever since their first contact. When, at fifteen, he'd called

the Parks' number—the aunt from California he'd never met—
he'd swallowed his pride forever around her.

I need you. Mom needs you, he'd told her, and then, there
they were. Widowed Tracy and ten-year-old Aurelie on his
doorstep in Freewill, Wyoming, in his house, in his life. He'd
never felt as much relief as when they had knocked on the front
door, and today, some of the same sense of relief seeped
through him as he focused on his aunt in the familiar yet foreign
setting of Heart's Anchor's kitchen.

"Do you want something to eat?" she asked.

"That would be nice, yes. Please."

Why did he have to sound so reserved and stilted with her?

Because here is the last place you want to be, a little voice
whispered in his mind.

He set out for the studio. He'd promised Jay he'd stick it out
a couple of weeks in Freewill, before he headed back to New
York and pick up with his life where he'd left everything. How
hard could two weeks be?

Chapter Two

"*I*s something burning?" a man asked from the corridor, the sound growing louder when Grayson reached the threshold.

Shayne looked up from the plate where she cut slabs of *badam barfi*. The cooked almond-milk-sugar paste should've taken more time to solidify, but thanks to the dry Wyoming air, she'd miscalculated the setting period, and thus found herself with a hard lump of dry, creamy-white sweet. Because of her lapse in judgment, she'd had to leave the pot on the stove unattended for a few minutes.

"Bloody hell!" What an idiot. No one left a pot unstirred when making Indian sweets. *Blast!*

She dropped the knife and rushed to the stove, where she grabbed hold of the wooden spoon in the thick, bubbling, crushed-gram mixture supposed to become *chana dhal halwa*, a hard yet chewy brown dessert served in cut-up slabs when cooled. After a quick stir, she crouched until at eye level with the blue gas flame.

Still too high. Shoot. Where the hell were her induction stoves when she needed them? She turned the knob, but the flame went out. When she turned the cooker on again, the flame soaring high and strong, she barely had time to lower the fire before a thick glob of cooking *halwa* bubbled up and hit her wrist.

"Oh, fuck," she yelped and tore to the sink, where she ran cold water on her throbbing wrist. *You should stop swearing.* Lord knew what sort of impression she was making on Grayson. He might be an arrogant and pompous arse, but she didn't have to prove how much of a harridan she could turn into.

"Are you okay?"

She didn't need an audience to witness her incompetence in the kitchen, much less him, the man she needed to impress if she were ever to go after him. *Get a life, you sodding cow!* "Yes, I'm fine."

The words came out through teeth gritted in equal measure due to annoyance and the lancing pain of the burn.

"Should you be doing something with this pot on the stove?"

She glanced up, first toward him still in the doorway, then to the pot.

"Forget it. The whole batch is ruined." The sigh escaping her sapped at the steel edge she'd infused into her shoulders.

"You can't save it?"

"No, I can't." Failure. If her teachers could see her. Hell, if her mother saw her. What kind of incompetent cook ruined *halwa*? A basic dessert, for goodness' sake, only requiring for the mixture to be stirred once on the fire. Even her father would be proved wrong. She didn't belong in a kitchen as he so often pointed out whenever she tried to take a step forward and do something with her life.

"There must be something you can do."

How many times had she heard the same statement coming from her parents? Nothing she did ever proved good enough. The burn of shame and the rush of ineptitude soared up, an inferno flaming inside her. She couldn't make a facking dish on her own here. She'd need more time, more help, more sanity not driven away by the god-awful dry climate that left her itching as if she'd happy-rolled into a bush of poison ivy.

"There's not a bloody thing I can do. Everyone knows it." Her shoulders sagged as the words left her mouth, and she pressed her hands down on the sink's edge, curled her fingers over the smooth metal, and let the cold weave its way through her skin.

"I think you're too harsh on yourself."

His voice came out soft, low. The gentle tone soothed her like a balm.

Shayne turned away from the sink and in his direction. He'd moved to stand near the kitchen table. She traveled her gaze over him, from his disheveled hair to the white T-shirt hugging his broad chest and the outline of the rippling muscles in his arms. She raked a long glance across the loose pajama trousers, to stop at the bare feet peeking out from under their hem. A different kind of heat seared its way up her body as she took in the casual ease in his stance, something which heightened his near physical perfection more than the tailored suit of the past day.

Blast it. A man who looked good in a suit and even better when he'd just woken up.

Trouble with a capital T.

All thought of burned *halwa* evaporated from her mind as she drank in the sight of him.

"You know," he said, "when something goes wrong, let it go and just start again. You can't change what's past."

"Is that what they tell you on Wall Street?"

"You heard I'm from Wall Street?"

"Aurelie mentioned it."

He etched the beginnings of a smile; Shayne waited with baited breath for him to smile fully, because just a tiny curve of his mouth looked amazing and promised a devastating sight when he'd grin.

"What else has she mentioned?"

His mouth didn't stretch, but when she peered up, the smile lay there in his eyes, in the small crinkles at their corners, in the slightly raised eyebrows as his irises shone with mirth.

Shayne ran the tip of her tongue along her dry lips. "She said this place is yours."

"Ah."

Had some of the frost from yesterday crept into his voice? Touchy subject, innit, his ownership of the ranch?

The jolt of realization that she dealt with a cold, pompous, and arrogant arse—after all, first impressions counted for something—zinged through her. She stood straighter and threw her shoulders back. Blast if she'd take the confrontation with him lying down.

"Listen, I know you don't like that I'm staying here. I'll move out; just say the word—"

"What are you talking about?"

At the frown on his face, her tirade died on her tongue. "You don't want me here; admit it."

"Why would I not want you here?"

"Hello? It's your ranch—"

"Run by my aunt with more competence than I could ever demonstrate. She's more in her right than I am here."

Wait a minute. That's not how an arsehole would talk. Definitely not with such an authentic note of sincerity in his words.

Had she misjudged him?

"I think we might've gotten off the wrong foot, you and me." He extended his right hand. "I'm Grayson Warner."

She glanced at the outstretched hand, back at his face, and the hand again. The nape of her neck prickled; she shouldn't touch him. Not if she wanted to escape unscathed. His touch would burn more than the cooking *halwa*, some feminine instinct told her. No possibility of being friends with benefits with this bloke. Benefits, yes, and a definite good time, in fact. Friends, no, because, then he'd worm his way under her skin and she'd be a goner.

"They liken me to a shark, but I don't bite. Really," he said with a small smile.

How could anyone not give in to the gentle invite in those self-deprecating words? Caution be damned, she'd take what she got from him. She was a big girl, knew how to protect herself.

Shayne reached out and touched her fingers to his.

Heat engulfed her, from her fingertips all the way through her arm, as he closed his wide palm over hers and anchored her hand in his solid grip. There existed no hesitation in his touch, which reinforced her impression that he was a man who knew what he wanted and who set out to get to his goal without letting anything stand in his path.

More trouble. She snuck in a small breath. He didn't release her even after a few seconds. His dark eyes focused on her face.

"Shayne, right?" he asked with his soft tone, and the hint of an accent.

He sounded faintly Scottish, without the rolling "r" in his words, but the stress definitely sat there on his vowels. Not the Wyoming drawl. New York accent, maybe?

Her hand in his started to burn. Something about his touch, being skin to skin with him, sent her pulse into a rapid thump, and she could feel the accelerated beat where the pad of his index finger lay against the throbbing vein on her wrist.

Double, double toil and trouble.

The opening words from Macbeth flashed in her mind. She found herself in a pickle, all right.

Fire burn and caldron bubble.

Fire definitely burned her hand, on the verge of consuming all of her if Grayson didn't remove his intense gaze from her face, from her parted lips. Caldron bubble, she had already managed, thanks to her burned *halwa*.

The cooking gram mixture hissed and popped. The sound tore her from the sensual haze around them. Why hadn't she switched off the bloody fire under the pot? Shayne pulled her hand from Grayson's grip and started toward the stove, but halfway there, she turned on her heel and returned to the sink. With a glance at him—he had propped a hip against the back of a chair and crossed his arms, dark eyes watching her with a narrowed look—she ran the tap and washed her hands. A different kind of heat, the mortifying, you-should-be-ashamed kind of burn, fired up her cheeks under his severe observation.

"It's nothing against you," she said. "I just, uhm, need to wash my hands before I handle any food. It's something my teachers always drilled in me, to wash your hands between cooking tasks if you touch anything not related to your cooking. This also helps eliminate the risk of cross-contamination in a professional kitchen and—"

She was rambling. Blast. She lowered her head to escape his assessing stare. Closing the water with a press of her elbow down the tap, she then reached for a few tissues and wiped her hands. She made it to the pot on the stove at the same time the mixture hissed and popped again.

Strong hands wrapped around her waist and pulled her back. She landed smack against a wide expanse of solid, warm male. The breath hitched in her throat, and she gasped.

Grayson's stifled curse sounded next to her ear. He released one hand and shut the gas under the pot. The mixture stopped bubbling a few seconds later, when he let go of her.

Shayne frowned as she turned to him. "What'd you do that for?"

He nodded at the pot. "The flying stuff would've splattered all over your face if I hadn't pulled you back."

Right. She glanced at the cooling *halwa*, then back at him. "Thanks," she mumbled.

"You're welcome," he growled.

He kept his focus on her, and she squirmed.

"You're not going to run under a shower because I touched you now, will you?"

Did she hear humor or hardness in his tone?

"Uhm, no. It's just," she faltered, "my hands I need to wash."

"Thank goodness." He leaned back against the chair and crossed his arms once more. "So, you're a chef?"

She nodded, unable to trust herself to speak. The warm imprint of his hands still rested on her skin, all the way through her sweater, where he'd touched her.

"You really can't salvage anything from the pot?"

The proof of her failure. She'd forgotten all about that, the thought obliterated by the sight and proximity to this hot and hunky man.

"If you smelt it burning all the way through the house, that means the mixture's ruined." She could transfer the top half of the pot's contents into another vessel and continue cooking, but she'd run the risk the dessert would have a faint burnt taste. Not something she wanted when out to show her competence as a cook.

"Doesn't smell burned here."

"Ventilation issue. Smells drift out when you don't have proper kitchen ventilation set up. Hence why I didn't smell the burning *halwa*."

"Burning *what*?"

"*Halwa*. It's the name given to some traditional Indian sweets, usually a paste of flour or mashed grains, cooked in clarified butter and sugar." She pointed at the pot. "This one's called *chana dhal halwa*. It's made with a paste of soaked gram."

"So, you're Indian?"

"Originally. Like, three or four generations back, my ancestors left India to go settle on a small island called Mauritius, which is in the southern Indian Ocean. My parents are from there."

"But you're from England."

"Right. Born and raised in London."

"So, what exactly are you doing here?"

Shayne tensed. Here came the questioning slant again in his words. "Aurelie and her mother invited me."

"I know this. I meant *here*, in this kitchen, right now." He waved toward the table laden with plates of *barfi* in different shapes and colors, bowls of puffy *ras malai* in thick milk cream, and small balls of cottage cheese *rasgullahs* floating in clear, heavy syrup. "What's going on here at four in the morning?"

"I'm cooking."

"I can see that. But why?"

Did he bite back a smile between these two sentences? Her hackles rose. Was he taking the mickey out of her? To hell with him. But she reined herself in. She better take her anger out on the person who really deserved it, not on a convenient substitute.

"Because Aurelie led me to believe she'd be helping me make those dishes. We have a presentation for Mrs. Harvey today, and I find myself on my own to cook everything. Thus the need for an early start."

"You thought my cousin could cook?"

The incredulity in his question scratched at the embers of her smoldering temper. The flames of wrath ignited and coursed through her. Bloody hell, she'd been totally conned. "That little piece of—"

Shayne bit her lip before the full curse escaped her mouth. She did swear too much, and who wouldn't, with a family like hers? Cursing turned into a coping mechanism in her world. But what an impression she must be making on Grayson.

"Hey, calm down, okay?" He shuffled over to where she stood. "If you need any help getting back at her, let me know. It's been a while since I've been able to play my role of big cousin properly, and I still have some strikes from Aurelie I need to retaliate."

Shayne's anger evaporated when she understood the true extent of what he proposed, and against herself, she laughed. "Remind me not to get on your bad side."

"I don't have a bad side. Not with good girls." He grinned.

Her stomach did a little somersault at his smile and those last words. Combined with the heated intensity in his eyes, there lay an invite to flirt if she ever saw one.

I'm not a good girl. The words refused to leave her mouth, though, because she'd be throwing oil on the blazing fire and roll headfirst from the pan into the flames.

"Do you want some tea?" she asked.

The grin faded, to leave a small, knowing smile tugging at

his beautiful lips. "Tea would be good."

She ducked from his side to move to the kettle at the other end of the kitchen. She busied herself with placing a tea bag in a mug and dousing it with boiled water. After bringing the steeping tea to the table, she cleared a space in front of a chair and set the mug down.

"Thank you," he said, and sat down.

The soft, breathless tone made her think of whispered words trickling over hot, naked skin with the feel of gentle caresses in the dark confines of a bedroom amid a tangle of satin sheets and downy covers.

Bad line of thought. She gulped as he wrapped his big hand around the mug's handle, to then bring the rim to his parted lips and tip the pale amber liquid into his mouth.

If that were her skin right there in the place of the mug's edge, her taste he let flow onto his tongue....

She forced her mind to snap out of the sensual thought.

"It's almost half past four. What are you doing up?" she asked, in an effort to steer the conversation to a less shifty footing.

"Already six thirty in New York, when I should be working," he replied between sips of tea.

"You start work so early? I thought Wall Street opened at nine."

"Wall Street opens at three thirty p.m. GMT, which is nine thirty New York time. And I don't work on Wall Street, which is for stock and stock broking. I'm into Forex. The Forex market opens at eight p.m. in New York, but London has already been up and running for quite a few hours. I try to get on the ball of the trades happening in London before I jump into the market from our end."

Had she understood more than two words from his little exposé?

He must've seen the confusion on her face, because he put his mug down and glanced up at her.

"Do you know what the Forex market is?"

She shook her head.

"It's an electronic marketplace where foreign currency is traded and exchanged. The market is active twenty-four hours, five days a week. The biggest markets for Forex trading are Tokyo, Sydney, London, and New York, each place with its particular business hours."

"So you have to be on the ball twenty-four hours a day to work in the market?"

"No. Most beginning traders make this mistake. There are times when the different markets' business hours overlap, and these are the best times to trade." He paused, eyes fixed on her. "Forex trades currencies in pairs, for example, the Euro against the American Dollar. You'd get the best trade for this combination, or even the British Pound against the American Dollar, in the time frame when both the London and the New York market hours overlap."

Shayne had never been one for mathematics and anything finance-related, but she found his explanation fascinating. Could be because she fancied the man rotten, but she wouldn't dwell on this small factor right then.

"Still doesn't tell me why you're up at four."

He laughed. "It's six a.m. in New York, and eleven in London. The London market has been at play for a few hours already, and I prefer to hop online to see what's been happening there before I jump into work at eight when the New York market opens."

"Oh." He must be a planner, meticulous, attentive, and definitely not impulsive. Here sat a man who must think everything through before he proceeded with an action.

Dangerous, because this implied his little invite to flirt earlier had been a calculated strike.

"Now tell me why *you* are up at four," he said.

"You said it yourself. Eleven in London. I'm not one to sleep in usually."

By eleven, she'd have had a whole kitchen buzzing and two-thirds of the lunch-hour food prepared and ready to go, back when she'd headed the Kadai Haveli restaurant in Southall.

"So you've come down and started cooking."

She nodded.

"Tell me more."

Grayson took a sip of his tea, not letting his gaze leave Shayne. This morning, he saw her without the rush and loaded reunion emotions of the past day. Try as he might, he couldn't get enough of watching her face and how her emotions played out so starkly on her too-sharp features.

Shayne Morea couldn't be termed a beauty by conventional standards. Her face, with its honey-gold skin, looked rather plain at first glance, especially with her black hair pulled back tight, until one noticed the spark in her liquorice-dark eyes, the ones that could flare into fire with a subtle inflection of her thick, well-defined eyebrows.

And when she stopped pursing her mouth, when she started to ramble and words tumbled out of her plump, full lips with liquid ease belying her clipped accent, Shayne proved to be an alluring creature indeed. He still remembered the feel of her curvy waist under his hands. Despite the thick sweater, he'd caught the softness of the firm flesh on her rib cage. He wouldn't call her chubby, but she wasn't skin and bones, either.

Ideal, in his perception, he who wished he'd lived in the *Mad Men* era just because the women back then could never be mistaken for coat stands.

Cut it, man. You're not here for a roll in the hay. Shayne deserved better. He had to take his stay here one day at a time. One down, fourteen more to go, so he'd get Jay off his back. He'd fib about coming to terms with the place and the memories, and get back to real life as he knew it.

And, he couldn't deny how Shayne intrigued him, a welcome diversion from the loaded memories the whole place carried. She tended to swear a little too much, highlighting his conviction Brits were either stiff upper lips or potty mouths, with no middle ground. Other than this, she had good going for her. Such as her dedication to her work. A little OCD—he hadn't forgotten the rush to wash her hands a few moments earlier—but must be a conscientious move for a chef. He liked to think he could trust the food he ate out, and for this, chefs would need to be stringent with hygiene rules.

He took the last sip of his tea and placed the mug down. Grayson allowed his gaze to roam across the overflowing table. Colorful Indian sweets shaped in squares, lozenges, and golf-sized balls covered an array of plates, and to one side sat big bowls filled with floating spheres of sweets in what seemed to be heavy syrup and thick cream.

The smell of all those sugary treats assailed him. He'd never tolerated sugar well, and even the scent could make his stomach roll. He'd chosen the wrong moment to come down to the kitchen. But he'd smelled something burning and worried how Aurelie might be loose around the stove, he'd come down, to find Shayne flitting like a butterfly between pots on the burners and plates on the table.

"Do you want some breakfast?" Shayne asked.

Grayson stood. "I'll grab something from the fridge. You're busy enough."

"It's not a problem, I assure you."

She smiled, and her face transformed like a burst of light illuminating her from the inside. Suddenly, Shayne Morea wasn't just intriguing to look at; she appeared nothing short of beautiful and breathtaking.

"You should smile more often."

She blinked, and now that he thought of it, she blinked a lot, as if a grain of dust got caught in each eye. A soft burst of color crept up her cheeks, and she lowered her gaze.

Hot damn. Given time, Shayne could all but worm her way under his skin.

Time he didn't have. Didn't *want* to have, in truth. Two weeks and he'd be gone.

The sound of hard heels clomping down the wood floor grew louder at the kitchen door.

"I can't believe you started without me!" Aurelie stormed into the room, stopping in front of Shayne with her hands on her hips.

"Like your skinny arse would've been of any help," Shayne bit back. Her eyes sparkled with anger. "Couldn't you have remained lost in your video game world or something?"

"I'm a game creator, Shayne. Of course I have to be in the gaming arena as often as possible."

Shayne snorted and turned her back onto his cousin.

Aurelie must've done a number on Shayne, and as much as he itched to know what brewed between them, he knew better than to stay in the same room as two women intent on scratching each other's eyes out.

He started toward the door, but Aurelie shot one arm out and bunched her hand in his T-shirt.

"Stay here. We need an unbiased third party."

"Unbiased, my arse," Shayne burst. "He's *your* cousin."

Aurelie brushed the words away with her free hand. "Whatever. I thought we were in this together, Shayne. How could you start without me?"

Shayne crossed her arms and leaned against the sink. "What would you have done, eh? You can't even boil a kettle of water without burning everything down. You brought me to this goddamn place on false pretenses, and when I find myself all alone in the lurch, you offer to help?"

Aurelie bunched her hand tighter on his T-shirt, the prick of her nails raking against his skin. His cousin turned to him, big gray eyes shiny with tears.

No. He would *not* get roped into their tiff.

"Can you believe this, Grayson?" Aurelie asked.

"Ladies—"

"Don't you dare drag him in so you'll have someone to take your side. I should just pack up and leave on the next flight out of Casper. Six hundred pounds never better spent, if you ask me!"

"Do you even hear yourself talk? You've been here for barely two days."

"Girls—"

"Two days too many! God, I hate this place."

"Then what the heck is all this?" Aurelie pointed at the laden table. "Why are you making all these sweets when you have no intention to stay and help Mrs. Harvey out?"

"Don't you bring her in here. I was stressed, and I cook when I'm stressed."

"You cook chicken *tandoori* and *kheema khichdi* and roll out chocolate croissants when you're stressed."

"Fuck you!"

"See? I know you all too well, Shayne Morea. You're not fooling me."

"Girls," Grayson said once again, but the two didn't respond. All the better, because he refused to be dragged into their impending WWIII. He took another step nearer to the door, but Aurelie pulled him back with startling strength in her thin arm.

"Oh no, you don't," she said.

Damn. No way out. He had to change tactics.

"Aurie," he said, reverting back to the affectionate nickname he'd had for her, "I'll be late."

She turned her striking eyes onto him, the narrowed stare pinning him into place. "Late for what?"

He had no clue, but he needed an escape route. "Late for going out with the guys to check the fences."

That amounted to the first thing to pop into his head. He hadn't been on a horse since he left, and he had no idea how the ranch hands and the manager worked in this decade, but cowboys went out during spring mornings to inspect the property's fence lines.

"I think it's a wonderful idea for you to go out and get involved with ranch business," his aunt said as she glided into the kitchen.

At quarter past five, the sun hadn't risen yet, and only a diffuse gray glow basked the exterior. Aunt Tracy came down dressed in jeans and a long-sleeved blouse, her long blonde hair coiffed in a bun at the nape of her neck. She stopped beside him, worked Aurelie's hand off his T-shirt, and clasped his upper arm. Her touch drifted soft and delicate on his skin.

"I'm so happy you're back and ready to get involved with the ranch again."

Grayson bunched his hands into fists at his sides. He didn't even want to set foot out of the house for as long as he'd stay here. But in trying to escape from Aurelie and Shayne, he'd dug a hole and thanks to the ill timing of his aunt's arrival, he'd have to dive in.

"It's your heritage, you know, what your family has left behind for you," Tracy added.

He nodded, not trusting himself to speak. The ranch, and everything reminding him of his family, of his past, of his father, represented nothing more than a dead albatross hanging from his neck.

His aunt released him and stroked his cheek. Under the gentle smile on her face, he didn't have the heart to tell her he had no intention of going out. Grayson bit the urge to flee, which left him to stand as a hulking piece of rock in the kitchen.

Aurelie grabbed his hand and pulled him to the table. He sighed and let her drag him. A part of him reckoned she'd sensed his demoralized spirit with the same sharpness a shark smelled blood from a mile away. But he had no energy to fight or protest. Instead, he braced himself for whatever his cousin had up her sleeve and which included him.

"So, we're taking the taste platter to Mrs. Harvey today?" Aurelie asked.

"I still have to make the *kheer* and *gajar halwa*, but the rest is done. Except for the *chana dhal halwa*. I burnt it."

"Cripes. What a shame. You totally rock that one."

Grayson kept half an ear to their sweet-as-syrup banter. What this what having sisters would've been like? Fights blowing up and peace blowing in mere moments later? Thank goodness he didn't have sisters. What ordeal would his life had been then?

Not any worse than what it's been. Probably would've been better.

He shook the thought away. Not the time to think of his adolescence in the big house.

"Shayne, is this buttermilk?" his aunt asked as she lifted the lid off a pan on the counter.

"Yes. I made *paneer*—" She paused. "Cottage cheese, for the *rasgullahs* and *ras malai*. Didn't throw the water away, thinking we could probably use it."

"Well thought." Tracy smiled. "Anyone want pancakes for breakfast?"

At the mention of pancakes, his stomach growled. Grayson sucked his gut in to try and stifle the sound. But he wasn't quick enough.

"Why don't you have some *barfi* or *laddoo*?" Shayne asked. "I made more than enough for the taste platter."

Exactly what he didn't want. He'd steered clear of Indian sweets so far, but seemed his luck had run out. How could he say no when three pairs of female eyes were on him? Expectation glimmered in Shayne's gaze, and loath as he felt to turn her down, he didn't want to disappoint her if he did taste her food.

He should've foreseen how his silence would've opened the gate wide for cousin-driven abuse. Aurelie picked a cream-colored, apple-shaped sweet from a plate and stuffed it into his mouth. Grayson had no other option but to close his lips and chew on the smooth, paste-like "thing."

"How does it taste?" his cousin asked.

The minute the sugar hit his taste buds, his stomach clenched and rebelled. But he couldn't spit the sweet out, and so found himself forced to chew and swallow as fast as possible. He achieved the feat two seconds later, still long enough for the roof of his mouth to burn from all the sugar in the little ball.

"God, I'm gonna need an insulin shot. Stat!"

Shayne's eyes grew wide. "You're diabetic?"

"No," he quickly reassured her.

"Then why...." Her face darkened as she let the words drift off.

How did he work himself out of this tight spot? "What are you planning to do with these?"

Aurelie snatched a golden-brown ball glistening with syrup and popped it into her mouth. Simply watching her down the sweet made him want to throw up.

"They're for Mrs. Harvey, silly," his cousin said. "We're going to teach her how to make Indian sweets so she can sell them at the Hometown Bakery."

"Lord, spare our townsfolk," he muttered, but the women must've heard him.

"They taste awful. I knew it."

At the dejection in Shayne's tone, he straightened. She stood with her shoulders hunched, and she had lowered her head.

"Listen," he started. "I wouldn't know because I've never tasted Indian sweets before. I could be way off track here. To me, that's just too much sugar in a single mouthful."

"Wait a second." Shayne looked up, eyebrows drawn. "You're from New York, innit?"

"Yeah."

"You've never tasted Indian sweets in New York? Hello? One in five inhabitants in that city is of Indian origin."

"Believe me when I tell you I've never had any Indian sweets."

Aurelie thumped him in the stomach, and he lost his breath for a second.

"Don't tell me you turned into a racist bigot on the Upper East Side," his cousin said.

What the fuck? "I'm not racist."

"Do you even know any Indians?" Aurelie continued.

"I do. In fact, my best friend is of Indian origin."

"Really? Is he cute? Single?"

He shook his head. The girl proved dangerous for any person's sanity.

She slapped him on his shoulder. "Come on. Is he single?"

"No. He's engaged."

The delight left her face. "All the good ones are taken."

"If this is the case, how come you've never tasted any Indian sweet?" his aunt asked from the stove, where she measured dollops of pancake batter into a frying pan.

Time to confess. "I don't have a sweet tooth."

"Nonsense. You used to love my pound cake and apple pie."

He gave her a halfhearted grin.

His aunt stood with her hands on her hips. "So all this time, you were humoring me?"

He shrugged.

She walked over, a dry wooden spoon in her hand, which she playfully whacked against his shoulder. "Silly boy," she said with a bright smile.

The sight reminded him so much of his mother the punch of a fist hit his gut.

"Okay, let me get this straight," Shayne said. "You don't like Indian sweets or Indian food in general? I thought New York existed as an ethnic-food capital."

"Just sweets," he replied.

Shayne moved to let Tracy use the sink. She pressed her back against the fridge and crossed her arms. "Name one ethnic food you've eaten and liked."

"Are we really going to do this?"

Aurelie poked him in the ribs with a long, pointed finger.

"Fine," he bit out. "Once, at Jay's place. His mother had made a little pastry puff. You pierce it with your finger before dipping in a dark sauce. I don't know what it's called, but it tasted very good."

Shayne uncrossed her arms. "*Pani puri.*"

"Right. That's what she called it."

She peeled her back from the fridge and shuffled her feet. "So this really means you don't like sweets in general. Not Indian food."

Looking at her, especially when she bickered with Aurelie, he'd never have pinned her down as someone who needed validation and reassurance. But what did he know; they were merely human after all.

"Right. I don't do well with sugar."

Somehow, he wanted to comfort her, to bolster up her confidence. He had a feeling the girl could go places, but only as long as she had people cheering her on.

People that included him?

He tripped on the thought, and watched as Tracy cleared the table and placed stacks of pancakes in front of three chairs.

Grayson sat and downed his breakfast, conscious of the liquorice-dark eyes following his every move as he measured out a teaspoon of maple syrup, which he drizzled on his pancake stack.

Shayne didn't speak to him again, and he didn't linger to start up another conversation. He had something to do. Something he dreaded, yet he couldn't worm his way out. With leaden steps, he trudged back to the studio and threw his closet open.

Not one pair of jeans in sight. The linen slacks were hardly appropriate for horseback riding.

He pressed his forehead against the closet door, let his eyes close.

Two choices lay ahead of him: chicken out of the outing with the ranch hands, or meet his future like a man and go down the hall to his childhood bedroom, where he would find an old pair of jeans that still fit him.

How much longer can you run away from reality?

Grayson stared at the insides of the closet without seeing the contents of the shelves.

Time's come.

Strangely, the thought echoed in his head in his father's voice.

He squared his jaw, closed the door, and glared at his reflection in the full-length mirror on the panel.

He was Grayson. Not Bobby.

And come what may, he'd do what he had to do.

Chapter Three

Should he be stoked how, at thirty-two, he could still get into the jeans he'd worn at seventeen? Years of hard partying with tequila, vodka, and beer, and he didn't have any more of a belly than when he'd been a kid. An achievement? Probably not, given how he'd failed at everything else where his aunt and Aurelie were concerned.

Not for here and now. He'd have to take it all one moment at a time. Such as getting used to those jeans again. He turned around, then took a step, and another.

At first, after he'd taken a deep breath and pulled the pants on, the denim had chafed at his skin, akin to a bad rope burn when someone was still learning to control a horse and pulled the reins too tightly in their grip. He'd stopped counting how many times he'd had to fiddle with the back of the pants, using moves not far from tennis champion Rafael Nadal's signature shorts-in-butt-crack adjusting. But the more steps he took, the more the fabric smoothed over his skin and merged with his movements in a flow coming naturally, like instinct. He'd worn jeans in New York, but here, in cowboy country, wearing denim proved a different, almost life-altering, experience.

It's in your blood.

The thought, once again, came through in his father's voice.

One final tweaking with the seat of the jeans in the privacy of the hallway and he dashed through the kitchen. Aurelie and Shayne were bickering again, their strident, raised voices audible from the stairs, and he wanted out of there as fast as possible before they roped him again in their little tiffs. Thank goodness the girls were in the dining room, and he zipped out of the house through the back door. He couldn't find his aunt anywhere.

Once out in the yard, he slowed his pace. The diffuse light of morning shrouded the surroundings, the sun's radiance floating in as if every few minutes, someone in the sky pulled a layer of gray same as one peeled a blanket from a snuggly bed in the thick of winter. The pale light cast a subtle glow over the estate. He stood grateful for this, because it meant he didn't have to take in the real physical extent of the ranch right away, the way the noon sun would've shone on every inch of the estate and extended the view all the way to the horizon.

The dry earth with its small pebbles crunched and rolled under the soles of his Nike sneakers. Damp, cool air surrounded him, and he pushed his hands farther into the pockets of his hoodie, bringing the lapels close together in front of him. The early morning cold didn't feel anything like the icy breaths of the wind in New York's winter, but the chill here in the Midwest wasn't something one could discount. Grayson inhaled, letting the clean air sear its way into his lungs and clear his head. What a far cry from the polluted, exhaust-smoke atmosphere in the Big Apple. He missed the smell of bagels and the aromas wafting out of the many coffee shops on his path every morning. He had a car and a chauffeur, but like most New Yorkers knew, easier to navigate Manhattan on foot and use the public-transportation system.

So the nearly mile-long trek from the ranch house to the barn didn't wear him out, because he'd grown used to walking every day. The jeans molded to his legs, folding into his step in a way his linen or wool-blend pants never had in New York. He frowned, refusing to contemplate if a meaning lay hidden in the realization.

The sweet smell of hay and horse, at first light, then pungent and dense, intensified the closer he got to the barns and the stables. Having grown up around horses, he didn't think they stank, what most of his New York friends thought. The distinctive scent of the stables—earthy, clogging, damp—settled over him with the comfort of a welcoming hug.

Damn it, what was happening to him? *You don't want to be here, remember?*

He stopped on the threshold of the stable, as if an invisible force field prevented him from striding into the darkened interior. Grayson frowned. The stable still looked the same as when he had left, yet, at the same time, it didn't. He had no idea who two-thirds of the people who milled inside the lofty structure could be, and from where he stood, he could hear many horses whinny, many more than the three mares in residence when he'd left. The ranch had prospered under his aunt's supervision.

A wave of shame rolled over him. He shouldn't have left her alone to deal with the property. He'd all but washed his hands of the ranch's business back in the day, and afterward, he'd never felt the desire to come back and see what went on. Even now, he balked at knowing, but he found himself on the spot, and only a coward would walk away. What would his aunt think of him if he did so today? So he forced himself to take a deep breath and step over the threshold.

Grayson blinked until his eyes adjusted to the darker surroundings. A few tall, stocky men fed the animals at the back of the middle aisle. Horses' hooves hit the ground in a regular, soothing staccato as they were led out of their stalls by ranch hands.

His memories, but multiplied five times over. He'd never seen so much activity in the stable early in the mornings. Late spring had reached them, and with snow not an issue any longer, the day-to-day running of the place required cowboys to hike out all over the property, start repairs on the field infrastructure, irrigate the land, and feed the cattle, until the animals would be moved from pasture to pasture in the summer.

He'd tried to forget all of it; in fact, he'd been convinced he had forgotten, but one step back into the thick of things and he remembered. Everything Mika, the wizened manager who'd handled the spread since before Grayson's birth, had taught him about ranch work came back with the speed of a subway train rushing into the underground tunnels.

Would he find Mika here? Still alive? He should know all this, have asked over the years, but he hadn't....

Grayson snapped out of brooding thoughts when his gaze caught on a scrap of a helper trying to haul a sack of feed in the far corner of the stable.

Goddamn it, they worked kids on his ranch? The little guy appeared as though he didn't even weigh a hundred pounds; how did they expect him to be able to lift that much weight around, a standard requirement for ranch hands?

He stalked to the corner, and his step faltered the closer he got to the kid, because "he" turned out to be a girl. Her short red hair spiked from a boyish cut, but the budding femininity on her freckled features could never be mistaken for an effeminate boy.

His protective instincts flared. Yes, girls made fantastic ranch hands, too, and he wasn't sexist. But his mother had always taught him to treat a girl with respect and deference, and to help in any way he could.

Grayson grabbed one corner of the heavy sack. "Let me get this for you."

She glanced up, and her green eyes—eyes he'd seen before—flashed with anger as she narrowed her gaze. She didn't release the sack, and instead, pulled with all her might.

"I can do it," she spat.

Great, what happened today? All the females on the ranch woke up off the wrong foot? "Sweetheart, you really should leave the heavy chores to the guys."

"Sexist pig!"

He released the sack. "Sorry?"

She stamped a foot. "You think I cannot work, just because I'm a girl?"

"I didn't say—"

"You did!"

"God, Marion. What are you doing here? You're supposed to be at home looking after your sisters," a man said as he approached them.

"I was minding my business when this sexist jerk here said I couldn't." She pointed a finger at Grayson, her green eyes still spewing venom.

"Who are you calling a sexist—" The man turned to him and stopped talking. His deep-set blue eyes went wide, and he turned to the girl. "You want us to be out of a house and my job? He's the ranch owner. My boss."

Did the man, whom Grayson didn't recognize, think him so much of an ass he'd kick them out upon a single biting comment? "Hey, I'm not this kind of employer—"

The blond man drew closer to him. "She doesn't know that," he said loud enough for Grayson's ears.

The soft tone and the manner this guy had of drawing close to speak to another? Only Jedediah Gilmore did so. Grayson squinted; could the big, beefy man be his string-thin, geeky sidekick from high school?

The girl, Marion, stamped her foot once more. "I'm not taking orders from Chuck Bass."

Damn, that awful name again. He bore a striking resemblance to the actor who played the part in a trendy, soap-opera-for-young-adults television show, but would the specter of the character chase him everywhere? He'd grown tired of the comparison in New York; wouldn't he be spared here as well?

"Who?" the blond man asked. "He's Grayson Warner, Marion."

"Whatever." She rolled her eyes.

"Now get out of here, and go straight home. Your mom will have our hides if she finds out you sneaked out."

She snorted and stomped out of the stable.

"Jed? That you?"

"Gray. Good to have you back, man."

Jed reached out and hugged him. With a hearty slap on Grayson's back, he released him. Unbelievable. Jed couldn't carry his school backpack because he'd been bony when they were kids. Who'd have thought he'd grow and fill out so much?

"Sorry about Marion. Got her mom's sharp tongue, I'm afraid."

"Who's her mom?"

"Lynn Miller." Jed grinned.

"The red-haired spitfire? Captain of the cheerleaders back in the day, right, going out with Dirk Bart?"

Jed nodded. "Dirk The Jerk. His loss, my gain."

"You're telling me *you* hooked up with Lynn Miller?"

"Been married for thirteen years and still going strong, with three gorgeous daughters." Jed grinned even wider.

Some things started to click. Marion had her mother's eyes. "Let me guess." He pointed at the door where Marion had left. "Your firstborn?"

"Bull's-eye."

The realization how his high school friend, the same age as he, had married and become the father of three plunged like a fist in his gut. This could've been his life...probably would've been, had he stayed. Married and a father. Who would he have gotten hitched to, though? Not Candace Sully, his senior year girlfriend, whose only goal amounted to exiting Freewill as soon as possible on the coattails of whoever could get her out of dodge. He'd figured that out when he caught her behind the bleachers with a jock who'd just earned a scholarship to UCLA.

The image of Shayne Morea's smiling face appeared in his mind. Yes, he could easily, too easily, in fact, see himself having never left Freewill with a woman like her at his side, standing together on the porch beyond the kitchen, gazing at a spectacular Wyoming sunset.

God, what was happening to him?

"So Wall Street hasn't made a nancy boy out of you, has it?" The man's voice sounded old and raspy.

Grayson turned to stare into the craggy, wrinkled face of Mika Bates. So the old geezer still hung around and had lost none of his sharpness in the past decade.

Mika grabbed the back of his hoodie and pulled. "Get out of these fancy city clothes; you couldn't wear a hat and a jacket like normal people? At least you got jeans on."

Grayson smiled and slapped the old man's shoulder. "Good to see you."

"You, too," Mika replied, his voice low and strangled. "Now get your ass in gear and come lend a hand. We don't sit around twiddling our thumbs while we watch a screen all day here, like you penguined-up hotshots from Wall Street do."

"I don't work on Wall Street."

"Don't you now?"

"I'm into Forex, not stocks."

"And that means"— Mika harrumphed— "whatever it means, when you're here on my ranch, you make yourself useful." He smacked the back of both Grayson's and Jed's head and walked away.

"Guess here's our cue to get to work," Jed said. "Still remember how to saddle a horse, Mr. Forex Broker?"

"You kidding? I could do it in my sleep." In fact, Mika had made them learn how to saddle a horse and mount blindfolded.

The words escaped him before he could think them through. For a moment there, he'd found himself back to when he'd been a teenager on the ranch, when everything turned out good and fate hadn't yet latched its cold, destructive tendrils on his life and those of his parents.

Jed smiled and thumped his back. "Just like getting on a bike again. You never forget."

No, you don't. And neither did you forget everything else....

ଓ

Despite Aurelie's incessant chatter, Shayne cowered in her seat. If she could roll herself into a little ball and disappear, she would. Her stomach did cartwheels, and cold sweat trickled down her back. They were on their way to present the taste platters to Mrs. Harvey, and she couldn't resist throwing glances at the many covered plates on the back seat. The bowls of dessert sat safely wrapped in cling film and stowed in the boot. Provided they didn't drag through potholes and over speed bumps, everything should be fine.

The light a few hundred yards from them, on the edges of the town, changed to yellow. Aurelie stepped on the accelerator and zipped the car through the intersection at the same second the light turned red. Shayne gritted her teeth and held on to the edge of her seat.

"Please tell me the light didn't have a camera that snapped our pic and that a Bobby won't come chase us down."

"Take a chill pill, Shayne. The camera wouldn't have had time to snap a pic, and you should see the cops here. Total hunks. It's actually fun to be pulled over, just so you can ogle them in their tight-fitting uniforms," Aurelie said with a wave of her hand. "And stop saying 'Bobby'; no one will understand your British slang here. A policeman is a cop in the US."

"Shut up." Shayne hissed while her heart kept up a rapid beat against the wall of her chest. When would they get to their destination, safely and in one piece, too?

Aurelie tore down the town's high street and screeched the car to a halt in front of a shop with clear glass window panels opening onto the pavement. The dark red awning above the window and front door had Hometown Bakery written on it in cursive reminding her of the piping of icing on a wedding cake.

Fitting for a bakery.

The contents of Shayne's stomach, which had soared up to her throat when Aurelie braked the car hard settled back down with a burn of acid. A hand clamped to her mouth, she extricated herself from her seat belt and slumped out of the car.

"Remind me to never get in a moving vehicle with you

again! This is reality, Aurelie. Not a virtual racetrack on *Need For Speed*."

Twirling the keys from her index finger, Aurelie walked around to the car boot. "Defensive driving is by far the safest way to drive."

"You're insane. Bat-shit crazy, and Lord knows what I'm doing here with you."

"You'll get over it." Aurelie plucked a bowl of *ras malai* from the boot and dumped it in Shayne's arms.

Strange how the milk cream hadn't sloshed out of the container, the cling film still a clear, unmarred surface where it covered the dish. If so much could be said of the other sweets....

The door of the bakery could be pushed both ways, so if one's hands were busy, say, with a big cake, the person could always use his or her arse to open the path. Shayne did exactly this. What a superb first impression she must be making, showcasing her jean-clad buttocks for the clients inside. But she couldn't let go of the gigantic bowl. Chefs should know how to cook for two, twenty, or two hundred. Shayne had mastered the twenty and two hundred part perfectly, but she had yet to make a dish that wouldn't turn out hefty enough to feed a family the size of Brangelina's for more than one meal.

"Well, well, well. Good morning, young lady. You must be...."

Nosy old biddy alert. Shayne's radar picked up the vibe with the same accuracy as when she stepped into an auntie's front room in Southall and London. She better brace herself.

"Shayne Morea," she said with a smile. "I'm sorry but—"

"Oh, so you're the chef." The old woman with the cropped gray hair reminding her of dull steel wool craned her short neck out, bringing to mind an android extending its X-ray vision onto the bowl she carried.

"Mrs. Flannigan, you will scare the poor girl. I didn't expect you so early, dear."

Shayne found herself having to stare down at the diminutive old woman who had ambled up to her. "Good morning, Mrs.

Harvey."

"Good morning, dear. I believe I told you to call me Evelyn."

"She's British, Mrs. H., and a stickler for propriety. She'll never call you by your Christian name," Aurelie piped as she came in, arms laden with plates. "Oh, hi Mrs. F. How's your knee?"

The Flannigan woman started on an endless roll of her arthritis, which would probably lead to her blood pressure report and diabetes update, if she had them. Didn't old aunts love to drone about their health woes, right before chiding their ungrateful brats of both children and grandchildren? Shayne ducked away.

"Sorry we're late, mam. Sorry, *ma'am*. Feels strange to say this since we only address the Queen as ma'am back in England."

Evelyn Harvey laughed. "What did you call me yesterday? Auntie, I believe? That should work fine."

A hot blush flamed up Shayne's cheeks. She hated being in a position where people were having a laugh at her expense. If she also thought of how Aurelie had conned her so far.... No, she wouldn't go there.

"We brought a sampling of most of the sweets I can make," she said. "Where do you want us to set the bowls and plates?"

"I cleared a table right in front of the window. We could display them there, and see if the people out on the street are intrigued or not."

Excitement pulsed through the old woman's voice. The way she couldn't stand still either made Shayne smile. All in all, it would be a good experience to teach Mrs. Harvey and her crew, even if she had to go at it alone.

While the three of them loaded the plates and arranged them on the display table, Shayne's focus kept returning to the thick gold band on Mrs. Harvey's left hand. She poked Aurelie in the ribs and lowered her head to her friend's ear.

"I thought you said she was a widow."

"She is." Aurelie threw a look over her shoulder. Mrs.

Harvey stood at the till, a few paces from them. "She lost her husband close to five decades ago."

"And she never remarried? Fifty years; she must've still been young when it happened."

"Barely in her thirties, so I've heard."

Shayne glanced back at the woman. "So sad. Guess it means Freewill has its own version of Queen Victoria."

"Who?"

She rolled her eyes. "The British queen, you cow. Ever heard of Victorian times? That was during her reign. She lost her husband and remained in mourning for him until her death, forty years later."

"Mrs. H. trumps her."

"So it seems." Shayne had to clam up when the object of their discussion approached them once again.

"These look lovely and delicious, my dears."

She smiled. "Thank you. You should try some."

"Oh, definitely."

The bell on the door jingled, and they all turned toward the tall, statuesque redhead who wrangled a waiflike creature into the bakery.

"I can't believe you dragged me here," the waif said.

"If that's the only way I can keep an eye on you, then so be it," the redhead replied.

"Humph!" The waif, who turned out to be a tween girl, snorted as she clamped her thin arms tight across her chest.

"Sulk all you want, but it's about time you started behaving like a real girl and not a tomboy."

A flash of memory zinged through Shayne. How many times had she heard the same line, or a variation thereof, from her mother when she was growing up?

"Good Indian girls don't play football like boys, showing no shame in baring their legs for all to see."

"A good Indian girl knows how to cook for her family."

"A good Indian girl is shameful and docile, otherwise she will not survive in her in-laws' household."

The remembrances flooded on the same stinging, acidic tone of her mother's stilted, accented English. Shayne blinked and forced her mind away from these thoughts. Her gaze landed on the sulking girl, and her heart went out to the creature. She could also see the resemblance between the two females; they had the same eyes. She would bet the redhead was the tween's mother.

"Lynn, there you are," Mrs. Harvey called out.

The redhead tugged her daughter in her wake and stalked up to them. She grabbed Shayne in a one-armed hug, held her fiercely, and released her. "Lynn Gilmore. I help out sometimes here. When Mrs. H. told us you were going to teach us how to make Indian candy, I just knew I had to be here."

Her bubbly manner proved contagious, and Shayne found herself smiling back when she stopped reeling from the surprise hug. She nodded toward the girl. "And who's this with you?"

"My daughter, Marion. I should never have named her for Maid Marion. She's got it into her head to be one of the Merry Men by joining the ranch hands now that summer is behind the door."

"You live on a ranch?"

Lynn exchanged a glance with Aurelie. "Of course, sweetie. At Heart's Anchor. My husband grew up there. We were all in the same year at school with Grayson."

"Oh." She'd forgotten Freewill amounted to a small town where everyone knew the other, having grown up together.

"Oh my goodness!" Lynn exclaimed and waved toward the laden table. "These look delicious."

"I wanted you to get here before we started the taste testing," Mrs. Harvey said.

"So what are we waiting for?" Lynn asked with a laugh. "But, Shayne, you better tell me what's what because I have absolutely no clue what all this is."

Shayne laughed too, and explained as the women moved from plate to plate. "The solid sweets are called *barfi*. They're made with milk and nuts"— she pointed at variations along the way— "the green ones being pistachio, white ones almond, and brown ones with cashew nuts. The small, apple-shaped balls are made only with milk powder and sugar."

"And what are these?" Mrs. Harvey asked as she picked a golf-ball-sized *laddoo*.

Shayne indicated toward the three plates with different variations of *laddoos*. "They're called *laddoos*, and these are sweets made with ghee, sugar, and flour. The dry, brown one is made with wheat flour, and the other, moist ones are made with gram flour or semolina."

While she kept the explanations flowing amid a chorus of oohs and aahs, she glanced at Marion, to find the tween standing in a corner. Marion had found an orange that she bounced off her bent knee like a footballer. Intriguing...*and even more like me...*

She excused herself and walked up to the girl. "You wanna try some of the sweets?"

Marion threw her a glare without pausing in bouncing the orange. "No, thanks."

Shayne didn't allow the negative vibes to get to her. She grasped the orange midstride, ignoring the narrowed look she received, and bounced the fruit on her own knee.

"Been a while since I've done this. I could go for three-hundred-and-fifty-seven bounces in the past. With a real football, though."

Marion's face brightened, and lost the pinched, sulking expression. "You played soccer?"

"Midfield, left winger. How about you?"

"No position yet. I was getting ready to try out for the team for the next school year, but we lost our coach and so we got no one to coach us."

"That's a shame."

"I know!"

She glanced at the table out back and turned to Marion.

"So your mum wants you to be a proper girl, huh?" She made "inverted commas" with her hands when she said the last words.

Marion shrugged.

"I know the feeling. My mum would pester the life out of me to get my act together, when all I wanted nothing else but to play football."

"Are you Indian?"

Stunned, Shayne stopped bouncing the orange. She grabbed it with one hand before it landed on the floor. "Why do you ask?"

"Because you remind me of Jess, the girl in *Bend It Like Beckham.*"

"You've seen it? Yes, I'm Indian, and first-generation Briton, same as Jess Bhamra."

"The movie totally rocked! Hey, I heard you're staying at the same ranch where we live. Think you might have a few free moments where you could teach me some moves?"

Shayne paused. She'd never thought she'd get roped into mentoring an impressionable child here. But what the heck? She'd been in Marion's shoes and thus knew the girl deserved a break. "Sure. Let me see how my schedule will be with the cooking lessons."

"Awesomesauce!"

Okay. "I better get back. You sure you don't want to come try a sweet or two?"

Marion wrinkled her nose. "If it ain't got chocolate in it, I'm not interested."

Chocolate *barfi.* The idea and the alterations to the original recipe popped into her head. Shayne smiled at Marion and turned on her heels to join the women. Her brain worked in overdrive to come up with a successful process to make chocolate *barfi.*

But all of it would hinge on Mrs. Harvey, and Lynn too, liking the sweets and wishing to continue with the cooking lessons. If her offerings hadn't won them over, she might as well pack and leave, ASAP.

She wouldn't have a chance to lend a hand to Marion, or to

get to know Grayson Warner better.

The two thoughts slammed home into her mind on the same rush, and the punch shot straight through to her gut. Wait a second; she didn't come here for anything other than teaching a few people how to cook. There shouldn't be anything else on her agenda.

Provided she'd have an agenda. All in due time, she reminded herself. First things first....

"So," she said as she stopped next to Mrs. Harvey. "What's your verdict?"

The old woman wiped her fingers on a paper napkin and clasped Shayne's arm. "You, my dear, have a magic touch. I cannot wait for you to teach us all how to make such delectable concoctions."

Slam dunk! Her next few weeks were sealed.

Which meant Marion and Grayson in her life—

Stop it! There's no need to panic. One thing at a time, take a deep breath, everything will be fine. She got involved in trysts all the time, had never lost her heart to any of them, and she had nephews and nieces she adored back in England. Nothing different here.

Paper bag. I need a paper bag.

"Oh, and just one more thing, dear," Mrs. Harvey stated.

"What?" Shayne asked.

"These sweets should be way sweeter. We're not going for the health-conscious here, but for decadence!"

 C3

Ten miles on horseback after fourteen years off a horse. Grayson groaned with every step he took out of the stable. Even getting down from the animal's back had been pure torture. He ached everywhere, in muscles he'd forgotten he even had. He closed his eyes on another groan, because he'd hurt even more the next day, when he wouldn't even feel what remained of his ass.

Mika, the slave-driving old codger, had wanted to put him in his place. Fine; he'd take his punishment like a man. But didn't mean he had to grit his teeth and suck it up. No, he'd whine and moan his way through the aftermath in the privacy of his studio, after downing a dose or two of ibuprofen.

And without an audience to witness his testy moves.

No such luck. He winced on the way to the stairs. The front door burst open, Aurelie and Shayne tripping into the house in a fit of giggles. At least they weren't fighting any more. For how much longer, though? These two proved as unpredictable as nitroglycerine.

"Grayson!" Aurelie tore down the hallway toward him, her arms wide open.

Whatever breath he still had left, after coping with the aches in his body, left him when she slammed into his chest. His cousin hugged him so hard her feet left the ground and she dangled from his battered neck. He brought his arms up, clasped her waist, and lowered her onto the floor again before she snapped his spine.

"Celebrating something?" he asked.

She jumped up and down, her booted heel landing on the toes of his right foot. He grimaced and moved his foot, all while he grabbed her shoulders and pushed her safely away from him. Damn, the girl could be a walking calamity.

"Shayne's gonna be staying for the next three months. Mrs. H. loved her sweets, and so we'll be teaching her and the crew at the bakery how to make them. Well, Shayne will teach them. I'm gonna make a vlog of the whole process and we'll upload it, kinda like a reality TV cooking stint."

Let's just say that whatever Aurelie had spewed actually made sense. The only thing he registered amounted to the fact Shayne would be there for the next three months. The whole summer.

What about him? How long would he be around? He couldn't afford to stay for too long. His plan spelled to come here, prove he could make it back to the ranch without a mental breakdown, then head back to his real life. The stuff of a few weeks, at most.

But "few" could mean two weeks, as planned, or twelve, about as much as intriguing and prickly Shayne would be staying over.

Damn it; he couldn't afford to think of such a situation. He had to get out of there, quick. Somewhere during the ride out today, he'd recalled thinking how someone could take a cowboy out of the Midwest, but none could take the cowboy out of the man. Being on horseback had been natural, even more so than when he sat in his corner office with the clear view of central Manhattan through its floor-to-ceiling windows.

In other words, dangerous. But at the time, he'd been stranded miles from the house, on the edges of the property, checking fences while Jed talked his ear off about his rambunctious daughters, the Gilmore Girls as they were known in town. Grayson had blanked the thought out, something he knew how to do very well, since back in the day when his father still lived, he'd made this technique his coping strategy.

He snapped out of his spell when Aurelie thumped him hard on his already hurting arm.

"Are you even listening to what I'm saying?" she asked.

"Sorry," he mumbled.

"Cut him some slack." Shayne stepped to Grayson's side and peered up into his face. "Why do you let her boss you around?"

"When you know my cousin, you realize there's less trouble this way."

"Hey, I heard that!" Aurelie whined.

Shayne laughed and stepped toward the kitchen. Grayson started up the stairs. Anything to get away from more thumps from his punch-happy cousin. With each step, he stopped feeling a little more of the back of his thighs. God, would he be able to hold for another dozen steps? If he made it to the second floor, he would be able to crawl on the smooth hardwood to his bedroom door.

The sound of a sneeze resounded, and another. Three in a

row. He stood on the middle landing, and when he leaned over the railing, glimpsed the back of the corridor and the doorway to the kitchen.

"Oh my God!" Aurelie exclaimed. "Is that blood? Shayne, your nose is bleeding."

Grayson froze. He could see Shayne where she stood. A ray of sun hovered on her; in the golden beam, dust motes floated in the air like mist. Dark red liquid seeped from her nose and turned her light pink sweater crimson.

He froze, his memories taking him to another time, to all those other times, when something similar happened in the house. In the final years of her life, his mother had suffered from recurring nosebleeds. Unresponsive and detached from the world, she wouldn't even realize when blood flowed down her nostrils and dampened her clothes. But sometimes, the thick fluid would slide down her throat while she remained prone and listless. "Gray," she would choke out in a soft whisper, and glance up, to try and find him. He'd remained by her bedside whenever he could during those last months, the only one who could calm her when she grew frantic.

The remembrance ebbed away and then crashed over him in an engulfing swallow. Suddenly, he found himself trembling on the landing. He'd lost his grip on the railing, and his knees refused to hold him upright.

"Grayson, do something, please," Aurelie begged.

She sounded panicked, and Shayne kept on sneezing, which would make her end up bleeding more. While most nosebleeds were benign, a person could lose a lot of blood if measures weren't taken to stop the bleeding.

With strength he pulled from Lord knew where, he tumbled down the stairs and stalked toward them. He had to take control; no one else would.

No one else *could*....

"Aurie, go get a clean towel and an ice pack." He grabbed Shayne's shoulders. She trembled like a leaf. Her eyes were wide when she lifted them up, telling him how scared she must be.

Exactly the way his mother had been. Scared, flustered, confused. He tamped down the swelling in his chest. Shayne and Aurelie counted on him.

His cousin came back with a white towel. He reached for it and pressed the bunched-up fabric to Shayne's nose. "Come," he said as he steered her toward the dining room, at the other side of the kitchen.

He made her sit down on a chair, and with his fingers on the nape of her neck, pushed her head forward.

"Shouldn't she be lying down?" Aurelie asked.

"No. If she's upright, the blood will flow down her nostril and not down the back of her throat."

"Euw, that is gross!"

"Shut up." The soft whimper came from Shayne. "Can't breathe."

Grayson squatted in front of her. For a second, he saw his mother's face there, but he blinked out of the memory. "You can breathe, only do it through your mouth."

He reached up and pinched her nose, just above her nostrils.

"Don't! Can't breathe."

His mother would also start flailing her arms when he did this, and he'd take the blows while he tried to restrain her. With aspirin from her cancer treatments thinning her blood already, they couldn't risk letting her bleed for too long. But by that point, she already lay lost in a haze of narcotics, and he'd often wondered if she wasn't delusional even when she cried out his name....

"Grayson," Shayne said in a strangled voice.

"Shhh. It's gonna be fine. Just breathe." He increased the pressure of his left hand on the back of her neck. "Lower your head. This shall pass shortly."

"I can taste the blood."

"All the more reason for you to lean forward."

Shayne hiccupped, and she grimaced, but in the end, she listened to him, and lowered her head. She took big, gulping breaths through her mouth, and he could hear when she stopped hyperventilating.

"Is she going to be okay?" Aurelie asked in a scared whisper.

"She'll be fine," he reassured. Provided the bleeding didn't last longer than twenty minutes, and she wasn't anemic, or taking drugs that thinned her blood. He'd done so much research on his mother's condition back in the day he'd debated applying to medical school. But if he'd have to watch people suffer like his mother had, day in, day out, when he became a doctor, he'd preferred not to choose the path of medicine. There existed more safety in numbers, in the workings of the market.

"Tell me when ten minutes have passed," he told Aurelie.

When certain Shayne wouldn't lift her head until he told her to, he released her neck. As his hand fell to her lap, she grabbed it and held on hard.

She had a strong grip, a little shaky still, but not the soft, limp hold he'd received from his mother.

Thinking of her made him ache with the suffering of losing her all over again. In New York, or anywhere else, the minute any unpleasant thought of her crept up, he could wipe the remembrance away and replace it with the sound of her tinkling laughter, the sight of her angelic smile.

But here, the memories had a life of their own. They behaved like catalysts, shot up all around him when he least expected, and affected him in a manner wrecking so much havoc onto his peace of mind.

Damn it. He'd come here for a new start, not to face demons at every corner and at every random moment.

He stood bigger than this though, stronger. He had to get a grip, right there, right then.

Stilted silence wrapped around them, broken only by Shayne's shallow breaths.

Grayson blanked his mind and waited as the seconds ticked by. He'd make it through.

Aurelie touched his shoulder. He looked up.

"Ten minutes," she mouthed.

With care, he released the pressure on her nostrils and peeled the sodden towel away from under her nose. A faint trickle of blood slid down toward her upper lip but dried up after a few seconds when he'd dabbed at the red trail.

Good. Ten minutes and the bleeding had stopped. Nothing more than an anterior nosebleed, probably brought on because of the Wyoming dry air. If she'd bled for more than twenty minutes, then he should've been worried. That could mean a posterior bleed, which would've trickled down her throat, needing cauterizing or a nose sponge at the community clinic.

"We should get her up to her room," he told Aurelie.

With a gentle grip, he took hold of Shayne's shoulders. Once he stood, he brought her to her feet.

She stumbled the minute she got upright, and closed her hands tight onto his hoodie to keep her balance.

"Don't let me fall," she begged in a small voice.

"I won't."

With Aurelie holding one of Shayne's arms, the two of them got her upstairs and into bed. Grayson sent his cousin to look for spare pillows, because Shayne should recline in an almost-sitting position. Once she came back with the extra cushions, he arranged them behind Shayne and pushed her back against the wall of pillows.

"You should rest," he told her.

He had the sudden urge to reach out and tuck her hair behind her ear.

He'd not even been able to offer his mother such a simple gesture of affection, seeing as she lost all her beautiful long hair to chemotherapy. One morning Grayson had come into her room, and her locks littered her bedding. He'd never wept harder than later that day, in the privacy of his room. His mother had needed him to be strong, for her, for everyone else. He had been strong, but he'd also been a seventeen-year-old kid who'd had to grow up too fast.

When he focused back on what lay in front of him, big, liquorice-dark eyes stared back at him.

"Where'd you go?" she asked.

Knives churned in his gut. Shayne couldn't know how, during her rare moments of lucidity, his mother asked him the same question when she lay on her deathbed.

"Nowhere," he gritted out.

"Thank you," she muttered.

He heard gratitude and something else in her tone, something he'd lost a long, long time ago: innocence.

No one should take someone else's innocence; it should be freely surrendered. His had been snatched. His mother's as well.

But not Shayne's. For a second, in his heart burned the strongest desire to see her smile and laugh, to be the person who made her smile and laugh.

His first instinct told him to flee, but he couldn't. His limbs had soldered to unmovable hunks of stone and steel, yet in his chest, the need and yearning hammered away at his consciousness until one thing only remained a certainty.

He'd make Shayne smile, and laugh, at any cost.

Chapter Four

Shayne turned once again in bed, willing sleep to come. The glowing numbers on the bedside clock read half past eleven. Already 6:00 a.m. in London, when she would already have been up for a couple hours. At six, she'd be sliding home into her loft above the restaurant, returning from the fishmonger and the greengrocers' after she'd picked out the day's fare for whatever they listed on the menu. She'd grab breakfast in front of the telly and hop down to the kitchens to start the day's stock of basic gravies and spice preparations.

Tracy had told her she needed to sleep after the nosebleed episode. A nosebleed, and the dry sinuses and nasal cavity leading to it, opened the way for viruses to easily get into the body, she'd said. Shayne couldn't afford to get sick, and sleep would help boost her immunity.

If only the blasted thing came when needed. She'd rarely required more than five hours of sleep, and in Freewill, she got her rest by napping in the late afternoon when her biological clock told her nighttime had struck in London. Which left her wide awake in the heart of the night, hearing every creak and groan of the big wood house when silence otherwise permeated the air. If she was a scaredy-cat, she'd say the house must be haunted. Something—what her Indian aunts would call *nazarr*, the evil eye—seemed to hover inside the dwelling. In the dark of night, the atmosphere hovered oppressive, as if something bad, like a malevolent spirit, lurked in the shadows, biding its time to jump on unsuspecting prey. She shivered. Her aunts would tell her to wear a black kohl dot on the outer corner of her eyes to ward off the threat, but she'd never believed such superstitions.

Thinking of the stifling ambience sent whatever rest she could've gathered out onto the strong wind that blew on the ranch at night. She sat up and threw the covers off, about to stand when the light on her cell phone screen, on her bedside table, came on. The sound of bhangra drums filled the air, and she clamped the phone into her hands before the ruckus woke anyone.

Only one person had this number. "Bloody hell, Dave. It's nearly midnight here."

"And how would I know that, eh? Where the hell are you?" her brother replied in a clipped tone.

"You're the genius, and you haven't figured out how a 555 number is from the US? I thought your bosses paid you to crack such information."

"Not anymore. I've turned over a new leaf, remember?"

"Right. Now you're paid to come up with the latest robot dog or robot cat prototype while you down sushi and sake by the buckets and chase after girls who look like they've escaped from an anime manga flick."

"Minus the boobs. Japanese girls are really not well-endowed at all."

"Watching Bollywood movies with the exaggerated *dhak-dhak* of those hefty bosoms has ruined you for normal girls, innit?"

"I can already tell you the girls in Tokyo are crazy."

"You can say this with such certitude after barely three weeks there?"

"Believe me, three weeks is more than enough to figure it out."

"Okay, so you called to discuss the lack of air bags on Japanese girls, or for another reason?"

"Just," he paused, "where are you?"

"Safe. Alive. In America." She frowned. Dave had never minded her business, which had made him the ideal big brother. "Why do you want to know?"

"Because Mum's been on my back all day trying to see if I knew where you are."

She should've known her mother would be beating the bushes to try and find her. The reprieve she'd bought with the note she mailed from the airport had dissipated already. Still, it took her mother three whole days before she started the campaign to find her wayward daughter. In the past, she'd pummel Shayne's door down if more than twenty hours had passed and Shayne had not given a proof of life.

Grimacing at the same time a shiver of dread coursed down her spine, she sighed. "I better give her a call."

"Oh, thank God. Please, sis, for the sake of my sanity, get her off my back. I took the job in Japan to escape the Big Brother lens she has turned on us at all time. Spare me now, please."

"Stop being such a drama queen. Goodness, you should've gone into movies, not electronics."

"Seriously, Shayne," Dave said in a calm, solemn tone, "you okay?"

She gulped hard. She'd give anything to have him hold her in his big arms, never having thought she'd miss Dave so much. But being practically at opposite ends of the world, Wyoming, and Japan, the sheer scope of the physical gulf between them sprang up and swallowed her. "I'm fine."

"You sure? Especially after...."

"My being here has nothing to do with him, I promise."

"Because that's what Mum, and everyone else back in London, is thinking."

"Can't they credit me with more good sense?"

"What exactly are you doing, wherever you are alive and safe in America?"

"Helping a friend out in my capacity as an Indian chef."

"You're sure there's nothing else?"

He could always read through her words, and see through her. *There might be a man involved.* "I needed to get away but not for the reason you think."

He remained silent for a few seconds. "Okay, I believe you. And between us, Pratik was always an arse."

Who'd had a very nice arse, she couldn't help recalling about her ex-boyfriend, a fact that had blinded her into not noticing the desperate crescendo of erroneous beliefs building around them. And then she'd seen him for what he was, a piece of fucked-up work, "Mummy" always the word with him. Too bad his mummy had been a sick witch.

"Whoever he's marrying," she said, "she's more than welcome to him. Poor girl, though."

"Nothing you should worry about." He paused. "Give Mum a call when you can, sis."

"I will."

"I'll call you soon, okay?"

She smiled. "Sure. Just remember you're fifteen hours ahead of me."

"Will do. Love ya."

"Love ya even more."

Shayne cut the call and slumped back against the sea of pillows on her bed.

No way out. She'd have to call her mother. Not from her phone, though, and not from a landline. With caller ID, her mum would get the number and Shayne would never hear the end of it. She'd come here to escape her overbearing mother, and she wouldn't hand over her hard-won distance so stupidly.

She'd need a computer equipped with Skype. Blessed be information technology. It made tracking easier, but with parents from the old generation who didn't know how to text or get onto Facebook, life proved easier for the likes of her who dealt with overwhelming relatives.

She got up, ditched the tattered old T-shirt she'd worn to bed, and changed into jeans and a light cashmere jumper.

Might as well head to the kitchen after she finished with the call. Chopping vegetables would be very therapeutic for the frustration any conversation with her mother would bring on.

The house lay still and quiet when she stepped into the corridor. Shayne couldn't help the shiver slithering along her back. Something weird, and not right, shrouded this whole place, and she grew attuned all too well to the hovering cloak, one that wrapped itself around her and made her glance over her shoulder as she walked down the hallway. The feeling settled around her, but her heart no longer hammered. A soft, soothing breeze blew in her hair, lifting the locks from the nape of her neck, and drifted away. Heavy stillness fell on the surroundings when the breeze left.

What on earth was that about?

She should be scared shitless. Her mind agreed with the rational conclusion, but something inside her heart made her certain she had nothing to fear.

Strange. She should ask Aurelie if the house was haunted. And speaking of Aurelie, she better go find the girl so she could get a laptop to call her mother. Dave would break under their mum's relentless harassment; with his hacking skills, he'd find her location within minutes and inform their parents. She had to ward off the possibility ASAP.

Aurelie would surely be in the basement, her gaming studio. The girl never went to sleep before three in the morning, if at all, when she got caught up in her RPG universe.

She made her way downstairs and pulled the door of the basement open. Sounds of loud crashes and explosions slammed into her, at odds with the quiet in the house. Shayne ducked down the stairwell and closed the door behind her, before the house's other occupants woke up believing an earthquake rocked the place.

Did Wyoming even have earthquakes? The question screeched into her brain, battling with the extra-loud gaming sounds and the solid vibrations pulsating off her whole body. How did Aurelie stand it? Thank goodness the basement had soundproofed walls; otherwise, the whole dwelling would shake as if a superpowered boom box resonated right along the foundations.

The farther down the steps she went, the more awe engulfed her. She stared at a veritable computer arena, worthy of the biggest tech labs on *CSI* shows. No less than a dozen screens covered a full wall. Each appeared rigged to display a feed from a specific program, but Aurelie had them all streaming images of the same video game, one screen making up a portion of the huge final picture. Aurelie sat cross-legged on the floor, a gamepad in her hands.

The final step creaked under Shayne's foot. Aurelie paused the game and snapped her head around to stare at her.

How did she even hear the creak of the step with all this noise?

The sudden quiet hit her as more deafening than the earlier ruckus, and Shayne reeled from the abrupt change in pitch.

"Sorry to interrupt you," she said.

Aurelie jumped to her feet. "No worries. I was just testing the new interface on the next demo version."

Her friend's high-pitched voice sounded overly loud. "You were playing against yourself?"

"Of course. How else will I test new games before I send them out to beta gamers? Better I find the bugs and glitches than a bunch of raving fanatics who'd tear me to pieces when I messed up."

Made sense. As the creator and conceptor of *Vanorra: Blades of Mythos*, one of the most popular role-playing games on the market, Aurelie Parks also held a superb reputation as a perfectionist whose game versions almost never glitched even in her test offerings.

"What are you doing here?" Aurelie shouted.

"Don't talk so loud!"

"What? Speak louder!"

She'd have more luck with sign language. So she mimicked a phone call, then drummed her fingers in front of her as if she pounded a keyboard. "Skype," she mouthed.

Aurelie grimaced. "You're calling your mother."

Shayne nodded.

"Take one of the laptops." Aurelie gestured to a table in the corner where three closed laptops sat. "They all have Skype, and the whole house is covered by Wi-Fi."

Shayne bundled a Dell laptop in her hands and made her way upstairs. "Thanks," she threw out before she left.

Aurelie had unpaused the game by the time Shayne hit the door; she closed the panel against the roar of a particularly fierce-sounding dragon and pressed her back to the smooth wood, the laptop clutched to her chest. Her ears rang, and she stumbled when she took a step into the hallway.

With quick steps, she reached the dining room and fell in a heap on a chair. After propping the laptop open, she accessed Skype and dialed the number for her parents' home. Seven a.m. in Southall. Her mum would definitely be up and ready to put up a fight.

The call went through, and with a quick glance at the screen to ascertain the speakers and microphone worked to optimum capacity on the device, she braced her back and waited for her mother to pick up.

"*Allo?*" the nasal, high-pitched voice sounded over the line.

Her mother never answered in English; she always fell back on the Creole way of answering the phone, just like she had back when she'd grown up on the island of Mauritius. Try as she'd wanted, Shayne had never been able to master the tongue, even though the dialect resembled French, a language she could bumble her way through.

"Mum, it's me."

"*Hai Rabba,*" her mother exclaimed.

Shayne winced; she should've known her mum would bring God in there, with theatrics worthy of a *Zee TV* soap-opera actress.

"Where are you, girl? Do you know how worried we all are? And didn't you think of what people would say? What does it look like when you disappear just when *he* is getting married?"

Ever since the breakup, her mother had never referred to Pratik by his name—always "he," or some other, derogatory, term. And of course, her mother wasn't worried if she was okay. No, nothing mattered but what people would say, and how they'd brush Anjali Morea's daughter as the talk of the town.

"Mother, I'm here for work."

"Work." Anjali snorted. "You had work *here*. Do you realize how you've let your poor Aunt Shilpa down? She trusted you with her restaurant. How many people would've given a newly minted chef the chance to run a restaurant kitchen? And here's how you repay her, by leaving on a whim?"

Lord, grant me patience and strength, and glue me to this chair so I don't go looking for a knife.... "The restaurant is no longer Aunt Shilpa's, Mum. She sold it."

"But she made sure you'd have kept the job, you ungrateful girl."

And sure, that's how I want to earn my job, by someone blackmailing the new employer to keep me on board. "Mother, I just called to tell you I'm fine, and I will be away for a few weeks."

Anjali harrumphed. "You'll be back when all this is over, and everyone will say you had no face to show for your shame while your fiancé marries someone else."

Here we go again. "He never was my fiancé."

"Oh, Shayne, don't be silly—"

"He never was my fiancé, Mum. You and his mother and every other aunt in the area jumped to the conclusion when he brought me to the *haldi* ceremony on the eve of his sister's wedding."

"And why does a boy bring a girl to a close family affair when there isn't anything serious between them, huh?"

"The whole of Southall sat there in their front room. How many times do I have to tell you?"

"For his mother, and for me, things were serious. You two were together."

My mistake. She'd also had the misfortune of sleeping with Pratik, and somehow his mother came to know. The batty witch raised hell because her son could only marry a "pure" Indian girl. And when Pratik had sided with his mother and all but fed Shayne to the wolves, she'd realized how much of an error she'd made in getting involved with him. For a while, she'd thought they could've had something, more than a fling. But this incident with him had convinced her she better never strive for "permanent," or even "long-term."

"You have to come back. Wherever in the world you are, you need to get back here so you can show the world how you won't cower in front of that *kaminay*."

At least her mother had called him a scoundrel. But no way would she go back. "I can't."

"What do you mean, *you can't*?" Her mother's voice grew shrill and seemed to pierce from the laptop's loudspeakers.

"I've taken a job here for the next few months. That's what I called to tell you." Her mother started to say something, but Shayne blocked her out. "I have to go. Just know I'm safe, and I'm okay. Good-bye, Mum."

She tapped the mouse pad and cut the call. Shayne took a deep breath, and the air came out in a snort when she exhaled. Why did it not surprise her if her mother had not even asked how she was? Anjali Morea remained more concerned about what people would say than what her children were going through. Shayne had not realized coming here coincided with Pratik's engagement announcement and his upcoming nuptials. The jerk, despite being blocked from her Facebook wall, had found a way to message her via the in box and tell her all about his future bride on the same day she landed in Casper. What an arse. What had she ever seen in him?

The quiet in the house wrapped around her, and the prickly feeling of being watched tickled the nape of her neck again. The "presence" didn't feel like the malevolent one, though, more akin to the gentle breeze that had caressed her hair.

Spooky. She closed the laptop and got up to head for the

kitchen, where she might as well get a head start on today's sweets. Yet, at one-thirty in the morning, she could roll out platter after platter of sweets until the time someone would wake up.

Grayson. He'd be the first one down.

A sudden urge filled her, and she blinked hard, turned when she felt someone in her back. Whatever stood there proved invisible, and the same kind of relaxed feeling she had around Aurelie settled in her heart.

Okay. So whoever her "ghost" was, he or she didn't spell out "evil."

Grayson. The thought once again popped into her head, as if pushed there. Could she be having supernatural intervention sending her into the ranch owner's arms?

Shayne would swear upon the thought that a low, tinkling laugh resonated in her head. Definitely a woman's, who sounded young and innocent. Another soft breeze rushed into her hair, and then she found herself alone in the kitchen, the stillness oppressing and subdued.

Her "ghost" tried to push her toward Grayson. Shayne bit back a smile. She couldn't deny her body's reaction to him, and she also couldn't forget the look in his eyes the day before, when he had stared at her from the side of her bed. For a moment there, she'd wanted to close her eyes and fall asleep, and still be sure she'd find him right there when she woke up.

Blast. She shouldn't have taken her tween niece to see the *Twilight* marathon at the cinemas the other month. She'd never seen the movies, and what wrong could there be in a teenage love story between a regular girl and a vampire? Except that shit proved twisted, because it made a grown-up woman such as her end up wanting to have a man watch her while she slept.

Even spookier than a ghost.

Being totally still in a kitchen made her fidget; she better get started on some food. What, though? She needed something requiring a lot of hands-on attention so she could work off the conversation with her mother from her system.

The clock on top of the fridge clicked on two o'clock. In two hours, Grayson would be up, and he'd need breakfast. *Pani puri.* The idea flitted into her mind, and she smiled. He'd said he loved eating that. It was the only thing she knew he liked and she could cook.

So she busied herself preparing the dish for him. Right, a snack for breakfast. But most people didn't realize snacks could turn into full meals if eaten in large quantities. This would be perfect for the morning.

She ducked into the crisper compartment in the fridge to find the ingredients to make the *pani*—the hot water sauce in which the *puris*, small puffs of fried dough, needed to be dunked in. She made the dough for the *puris*, and after pulling small balls and flattening them with a rolling pin, she placed the disks between two damp towels, in order to keep them moist and ensure they'd puff up once she fried them in hot oil. Both the *puris* and the *pani* were best made right before eating, so after a quick glance at the clock, which indicated barely three, she set aside what she had already prepared and pulled out rice, ground meat, and the other ingredients necessary for making *kheema khichdi*, her favorite fix in times of crisis. Just like some people ran or kicked a punching bag to alleviate their stress, Shayne cooked some comfort food staples such as the *khichdi* and brought her blood pressure down by eating the dish and savoring each spoonful.

She kept glancing at the clock while she sliced the onions and fried them, then chopped the coriander and mint required for the dish. The black lentils, which the shopkeeper in Casper, the closest big town with a shop selling Indian staples had assured her, were quick-cooking, soaked in a bowl next to the Basmati rice. At quarter to four, she left the preparations for the *khichdi* behind and started the burner under the pan with four inches of vegetable oil in it. A few minutes later, she began frying the flat, rolled-out *puris* in batches of five. The pastry puffed up after ten seconds in the oil, and they were crisp and golden when she spooned them out onto a paper towel.

Shutting the burner under the oil, she went to prepare the *pani*. Shayne found an old blender in one of the cupboards. After washing out the jug, she threw in the tamarind paste, mint leaves, green chili, and salt for the *pani*, and started the blender. The motor revved up once, twice, and then made a clogging sound. Sparks erupted where the power cord left the base of the motor.

Strong arms wrapped around her waist and pulled her back.

"Why are you so intent on getting into trouble anytime I'm not around?" Grayson asked, a hint of humor in his voice.

She lay with her back flush against his chest. His warmth spread out to her. She tilted her head up, to stare at his well-defined jawline, before he, too, inclined his face and peered down at her.

Something hard crept up his features, shuttered his gaze.

"What are you doing down here? You should be resting after yesterday."

She should've told him something along the line of, *"You're not my mother"*; no one got away addressing her so. But the words that left her lips sounded like, "I made *pani puri*."

Tinkling laughter rang like a long-lost echo in her mind, and she froze. The ghost came back?

"Is the house haunted?"

He narrowed his eyes and released her slowly. Probably thought her stark-raving mad, or one of those sensitive Britons who saw ghosts everywhere.

"Sorry?" he asked.

At the incredulity in his voice, Shayne snapped out of the spell that had fallen over her. She drew to her full height, straightened her spine, and stepped away from him. "Never mind."

She turned away and busied herself with draining the water from the soaking lentils.

"Where did you find this relic?" Grayson asked.

She glanced his way. He pointed at the old blender. "Oh, that. I needed to make a paste for the *pani*." *Which reminds me*.... Silly she had left the task unfinished.

"Don't use it. The power supply short-circuited."

Hence the sparks when he'd pulled her back. Somehow, she could've sworn those sparks had shot off something else, like her skin.

"I still need the jug."

He wrapped his large palm around the handle and dislodged the jug from the base. She grabbed it with both hands around the clear plastic when he held it out to her, careful not to let her fingers touch his.

"What are you making?" he asked.

"*Pani puri.*"

"Huh?"

Oh no, he wouldn't do this to her. "You said you liked eating that."

"I'm sorry, I don't—"

"Oh, just shut up, will you?" He clearly had no clue what she talked about, and since actions spoke louder than words, she better show him what she meant.

She pulled a chair at the table, threw him a scathing glance, and took the jug to the counter, where she emptied the contents into a sieve. The ingredients hadn't had time to become a fine paste, but they had mixed; she needed nothing more. Shayne stirred two cups of water into the green-brown mixture and collected the *pani* sauce in a large bowl underneath. She tasted it for salt and hotness, then spooned a little in a small bowl, which she took to Grayson with a plate of puffed-up *puris* in her other hand.

"This is what you ate at your Indian friend's place, innit?"

He gave her a sheepish grin. "Yes."

He really had a wonderful smile. When he looked at her this way, like a mischievous boy who'd been caught with his hand in the biscuit tin, she couldn't stay angry at him. Lightness swept through her, and she smiled back.

"Go on, eat," she urged, with a nod toward the *puris*.

He picked up a small dough puff, and when he pushed his

thumb into it, the whole thing crumbled in his hand.

Grayson cursed, and she laughed. Obvious he wasn't Indian, not by a long shot. "Use your little finger, silly. Like this."

She grabbed a *puri*, pricked it with her little finger so only a small hole dented the puff, then dunked the whole thing into the spicy *pani*. The hollow *puri* would fill up with the watery sauce, which would explode on the taster's tongue when he ate it.

She brought the *pani puri* in her hand up.

In a flash, his eyes darkened, and he wrapped his fingers around her wrist. Slowly, he tugged her hand closer, and he opened his lips, took the pastry from her and into his mouth. His soft lips grazed her skin, and he didn't let her pull back while he savored his *puri*, and swallowed.

"Delicious," he said softly.

Shayne sucked in a breath. His eyes were hooded, jaw tense, and a small smile hovered on his lips.

"You like?" She sounded breathless, her voice so low it could've been another woman who spoke.

"I like a lot," he replied just as low.

He still held her wrist, and without releasing her, he stood.

With a single tug, he could reel her to him. She wanted nothing more than to be flush against him, to have his wide, warm body on hers.

Pull me to you. Dare she ask it aloud, though? She could be brazen, yes, but so soon, and with a man she barely knew? She debated the question in her mind, in those split seconds that could've lasted an eternity, until he broke the quiet.

"Come with me."

Chapter Five

"What?" Shayne gasped.

Grayson nodded in her direction. "Is this thing on you warm enough?"

"You're not making any sense here."

Notions of heat and desire battled with confusion, and she could only stare at this man who sounded as though he knew what he spoke about. Good thing at least one of them did.

"Come on," he said with a little smile and tugged her toward the back door.

On the way, he grabbed a thick jacket off a peg on the wall and released her hand while he slipped the garment on. Grayson picked up a puffy anorak, which he settled on her shoulders.

He focused those dark chocolate eyes on her, and she found herself pinned to the spot.

"Come," he again said, hand extended.

If he bid her follow him to Hell right that moment, she would've acquiesced and gone ahead. Compulsion laced the one word, and she wondered if normal men could compel a woman to do their bidding, all through their voice. Just like vampires. Blast it, she shouldn't have gotten sucked into the vampire pop-culture madness.

"Where"— her tongue had glued to the roof of her mouth—

"are we going?"

"I'll show you."

What else will you show me? Bloody hell. Could somebody pack so much sexual innuendo into a sentence with such effortless ease?

He grasped her hand again, laced his fingers with hers. His touch felt solid, as if it belonged there; perfectly natural.

Warning bells, girl, these are warning bells! But heck if she wanted to heed them.

He pulled, and she went. Out the back door, onto the porch, down the steps, until they stood on the wide expanse of land between the house and the barn and stables, located about a mile from the main ranch house.

A thin cloak of mist shrouded the surroundings. All around them, the air appeared pale, hovering between night and dawn. A silvery-gray glow cast its subtle radiance on the land. Wherever Shayne glanced, empty plains stretched to the horizon.

"It's beautiful." Releasing his hand, she turned in a full circle, letting herself drink in the feel of this majestic land. Hate the place as she might, she had to admit wild beauty existed in the rough landscape of Wyoming.

"Take a deep breath."

"Huh?"

"Go on." He dipped his head toward hers.

The words flew out of his sensual lips to settle akin to the soft trickle of thinned honey over her skin. Shayne couldn't help herself; she gasped, and in the process, hitched in a big gulp of air.

Strange how her throat didn't start itching, and her nose didn't burn. Neither did her eyes feel gritty out here.

She blinked up with surprise into Grayson's face, especially when he smiled.

"I knew it'd do you good. The morning air is more humid than what you've been used to."

Yes, the atmosphere did seem heavier than during the day,

or even the evenings. She took in another deep breath, through her nose, and the telltale moisture she always drunk in back in England coated the inside of her nostrils and seeped through to her lungs.

Her breathing quickened.

"Okay, don't start hyperventilating yet," Grayson said on another chuckle. "The air's not going anywhere."

Humor laced his words. She loved the way the lightness of the moment settled on his features and made the corners of his slanted eyes crinkle from his smile.

Goodness, he was gorgeous. She shivered as the full force of his attraction slammed into her. Dangerous, sinful, decadent, like downing death-by-chocolate ASDA mousse cake in between shots of ice-cold vodka. She always felt crappy the next day, swore she'd never gobble such a lethal combination of food ever again, but who was she kidding? She'd go back for second helpings, thirds, even fourths.

And she had a feeling that with Grayson, if she took one bite, she'd be a goner.

She shivered again when the realization slithered down her spine.

Grayson frowned and drew closer.

Move away; don't come any nearer!

He brought his hands up and clasped her shoulders. Even through the padded anorak and the cashmere jumper, she could imagine the heat from his touch sink into her skin and spread with the comfort and bliss of a soothing balm.

Bloody hell, girl. You're not here to land in a man's bed, certainly not this man. You know you'll be toast if you give in to him.

"You're cold?"

Another trickle of honey down her whole body. *Blast.* "I...I'm fine."

"You busy back in the kitchen?"

Like a dimwit, words failed to come out of her mouth, because he stood so, *so* close to her. If she took a deep breath, her anorak-padded chest would brush against the soft suede of his jacket.

He released her shoulders. With his hands gone, the heat left her and the surrounding cold snuck in and wrapped itself around her.

"Put your hands in the front pockets," he said. "We should get you moving again; you're not used to this morning cold. Let's take a walk?"

She acquiesced with a nod.

When he started in the opposite direction from the house, she threw a quick glance at the dwelling. She should go back in, get on with her cooking, and leave Grayson Warner as far behind her as she could.

But drat if the sensible side of her brain could overcome the romance-starved part of her whole being hunkering for attention and affection, preferably from the man right here.

"You coming?" he asked as he stopped a few feet from her.

Turn tail and head back in.

"Yes." They fell into step, and comfortable silence settled between them as they made their way down the path.

At one point, Grayson snorted with laughter.

"What's so funny?"

"You've taken more steps outside than I've ever gotten Aurelie to take in all our time here."

"But I thought she haunted the stables. Seemed to me she went everywhere on horseback."

He laughed again. "She gets someone, usually a ranch hand, to take her to the stables in a truck. I swear, if we lived in old times, she'd have a horde of servants carry her everywhere on one of those stretcher-type carriages."

"A palanquin, you mean." Shayne laughed and the humor died when she felt his intense stare on her.

"You're not afraid of walking, are you?" he asked.

"Not at all." She kept her eyes focused on the structure in the distance. Still a tiny speck on the horizon, but she'd bet she would find a barn painted bright red. "I'm from Southall."

"And?"

She bit back a laugh at the confusion wrinkling his forehead.

"All right. So since you're from New York, how do I explain it best? You know how there's Little Italy over there?" She caught his nod. "Well, Southall is the Little India of London. Thank goodness, not polluted and crowded like India, but the shops, the lifestyle, the people? You'd be hard pressed to realize you're actually in modern England. And the roads are always clogged with cars in Southall, because everyone wants the neighbor to know he has a better car and show off. Trust me, you're better off going where you need to on foot."

"A lot like Manhattan, then."

"I suppose."

"You've never been to New York?"

"Nope."

"I might have to invite you over, in that case."

Another incitement to jump with eyes wide open into the slack jaw of a drooling Hellhound.

One she wouldn't dream of refusing.

Blast!

And shoot if the air between them didn't charge up with electricity and tension. It bristled along her arms, stung her face with heat. She had to bring things back onto neutral ground, quick.

Shayne nodded at the structure a few hundred yards away. Definitely a barn, painted red. Low-ceilinged stables stood next to the wood building. "We're heading there?"

The smell of hay, and horses, assaulted her nostrils. The place stank, but the scent didn't strike her as so bad after a few breaths. Quite earthy, rich, and dense. At least, she couldn't smell any muck or horse shit around, a surprise, considering how the mews still used as stables back in England stank to high heaven of horse poop.

"And you haven't fainted yet from the smell," Grayson said. "Thank God you didn't prove me wrong here."

"I beg your pardon?"

"It appears every city girl who comes close to a stable falls unconscious before even stepping foot inside from the smell alone. I thought you'd be strong and capable, and you didn't prove me wrong."

"Seriously? I'm not a city girl, though."

"You're not a Midwest cowgirl, either," he said. "Yet."

What did he mean by these words?

They'd reached the entrance of the stable. A craggy-looking, wizened man with a weather-beaten face started in their direction.

"'Didn't wuss your way out of another day of work, I see," he said with a nod toward Grayson. He stopped a few paces from them and tipped the edge of his hat. "Ma'am."

Shayne smiled at him. "You know you just addressed me like we address the Queen?"

"Eh?" The old man squinted.

"Back in England. The only one addressed as Ma'am is the Queen."

"Ack. You not some high-handed colonist Brit, are ye?"

"Mika, cut it out," Grayson said. "She's our guest."

Shayne peered from one man to the other. "It's okay. I'm not at all a colonist. In fact, I'm of Indian origin, which would make me as much a former subject of the Empire as the Americans."

Mika tipped his hat again. "I like the sound of this, missy. So, a guest, eh?"

Grayson shifted from one foot to the other under the old man's pointed stare. "She's Aurelie's friend, here to help the folks over at The Hometown Bakery with some cooking lessons."

"You not crazy like that girl, are ye?"

"Uh, not that I know of," Shayne replied.

"Good. 'Cause she's gonna give me a heart attack before it's my time to go join the good Lord. And you a cook or something?"

"She's a chef," Grayson said before she could answer.

"The ones who make those fancy-looking plates with food to feed a kitten and never enough to fill a grown man's belly?"

Somehow, it felt as if she stood on the stand here, with Mika being judge and grand jury rolled into one. Her acceptance onto the ranch seemed to hover a lot on the old man's blessing. "I make a mean roast, with all the trimmings. And you should try my steak-and-kidney pie."

"Blessed be the Lord! Ye're a good sort, missy, that ye are. Want me to saddle up a horse for ye?"

She caught the expression of surprise on Grayson's face, but she had to shrug it off when Mika's question settled in. "Uh, no. Thanks."

"Ye afraid of horses? Nothing to be scared of."

"I'm not. It's just...." She gulped.

"What?" Grayson asked.

Time to tamp down the embarrassment flaring up on her previously cold cheeks. "I've never been on a horse."

"Ha! And ye're from England? I thought all Brits learned to ride before they could run."

"Only if you're from the royal family or their entourage," she corrected.

"Never mind. We'll have ye on horseback and riding like a real cowgirl in a jiffy. Won't we, Grayson?"

Shayne glanced again from one man to the other, trying to figure out the unspoken message passing between them.

"Seeing as Grayson is not helping any around here by hauling his ass in to work with the hands, he could teach you."

"No. Wait a second—"

"I'd be glad to show you."

Grayson's calm, assured tone stopped her short.

"How about now?" Mika piped up.

"No." She shook her head, trying to come to grips with the situation and how these two blokes had run over her with their plan. "I have stuff on the cooker in the kitchen. Today is not a good time."

"Never" would work as the best time, too. She had to get out of this, fast.

"Speaking of stuff on the cooker, I'd better go back," she added.

Mika chuckled. "Ye not running away, are ye, missy?"

"Surely not!" Heat flamed on her face again.

"Then how about tomorrow morning, same time, ye get down here and let Grayson take ye out on yer first lesson?"

As much as it pained her to concede defeat, she'd backed herself into a corner and had no way out. She stuck her hand out. "Deal."

Mika took her hand in his weathered palm and gave a strong squeeze, nearly crushing her bones. The man appeared as thin and dry as a piece of jerky. Where did he pack such strength in his wiry body?

"I better go."

Mika released her hand and tipped his hat. "See ye tomorrow, missy."

She started out of the stables, then paused when Grayson didn't follow. Shayne turned to him. A serious frown scrunched his features.

He'd been played by the old geezer as much she. She'd bet he had no desire to teach her how to ride.

There had to be a way to worm out of the situation. Maybe if she slept in tomorrow morning? No, not a solution. Her internal clock already off, she'd set herself for a bout of bored madness if she failed to come down in the morning.

Grayson's cell phone rang, the shrill ringtone slicing through the air with a jolt that shocked both of them.

He pulled the device from his jeans pocket. "I have to take this. You better go ahead to the house. I might take a while."

She nodded, relieved to be alone with the tempestuous thoughts rumbling in her head. The clean, damp morning air might help her clear the fog out of her brain.

On the doorstep, she turned back to him. "You haven't had any breakfast yet."

"I'll be in shortly."

"Okay."

She moved out of the stable and up the path, returning to the ranch house. Her feet couldn't carry her fast enough, and she almost ran all the way back. Her heart hammered against her rib cage—did that come from her rapid pace, or from the maelstrom of emotions churning inside her?

One thing she did know, though. Grayson Warner would be dangerous for her, and the less distance between them, the more she stood the chance of losing herself to him.

Shayne closed her eyes tight once she stepped onto the back porch.

Aurelie had said Grayson wouldn't be staying for long. She prayed her friend was right, and Grayson left as soon as possible.

Grayson watched her departing form from where he stood, rooted to the spot, inside the busy stables. In his hand, the phone continued to screech, but he couldn't bring himself to answer just yet. No, he wanted to keep staring at her, at the same time he didn't want to acknowledge the speed in her step, as if she couldn't wait to get away from there.

From him.

Damn Mika for putting them on the spot in such a tricky way. The old codger had all but toyed with her like a cat playing with a mouse, before he grew disinterested in the game and pawed the small, defenseless animal to another, more dangerous cat. In other words, him.

When the phone didn't stop ringing, he answered. "Hi, Jay."

At the other end of the line, Jay Elliott whistled.

"Should I have hope you're not suicidal or homicidal yet? Two days back in Freewill and you didn't bite my head off when you picked up."

"Fuck off." What did his meddling best friend want?

Jay chuckled. "That's more like it."

Grayson didn't reply. He started out of the stables and up the path back to the house. His stomach cramped, reminding him he'd yet to have any food this morning. Except for the one *pani puri* he'd grabbed from Shayne's fingers. He didn't have to close his eyes to remember the look on her face when he had held her wrist and pulled her hand toward his mouth. Damn if he hadn't seen heat flare up in her dark eyes, in the flush painting her golden cheeks—the color of creamy peanut butter—a light shade of crimson.

And the taste of her skin. Warm, salty, sweet, with a hint of herbs reminiscent of minty soap. Shayne had short nails, and he'd sucked the whole tips of her fingers into his mouth, closed his lips on her smooth flesh.

"Gray? You listening to me?"

He snapped out of his memories. "You're gonna have to repeat that."

"I was just asking how you were doing."

"That's rich, coming from the guy who all but slammed me down here and left me no other way out."

"It's for your own good. You know this; I know this. So how about we stop skirting around the issue and just face it like grown men?"

"Fuck—"

"Off. I know! Anything else new?"

The fight left Grayson, and he breathed out. Jay was right. How long did he think he could cope without facing his demons? Better now than later, when he'd have made a mess of his life, and his clients'.

"Things could be better," he confessed.

"But you're holding up?"

"Yeah."

"I always knew you had it in you, man."

His throat clogged at the quiet confidence and obvious brotherly fondness in Jay's voice. Thank goodness for good friends; otherwise, they'd all be screwed.

"How's the market looking?" He shifted the topic, before he blurted out something sappy and made a fool of himself.

"Not bad. Everything's holding up, even with you away."

Jay's words held heavy humor.

"You and Robin are more than capable of holding the fort." *And it's only for two weeks.* But he didn't add this last part. Something held the words back, something he didn't want to acknowledge just yet.

"Speaking of the fort, it's the reason I'm calling."

"What's the matter?" Grayson straightened at the same time he slowed his step, focusing his attention on what his friend would say next.

"I need to leave the office for a few days with Robin."

"Why?" Damn, this didn't sound good.

"Eriadne left for Milan yesterday—"

"Without telling you, I bet." Grayson delivered the words in a cool tone, unafraid this time to stare at the truth in the face and force Jay to meet with it like a man, too.

Jay remained silent.

"Speaking of Eriadne, when's the wedding again?" Catty of him, low and base, as well, but he had to make Jay see sense. Something his friend wouldn't as long as the Victoria's Secret Angel held him by the balls.

"Now you sound like my mother."

"Aunt Lilette is right, you know. You've been engaged for over a year, and Eriadne keeps putting off the conversation about the date. I thought all girls were impatient to get their big day."

"Man, listen," Jay started. "I've got to give us a chance."

"You've been giving Eriadne Bellefort chance after chance for the past three years. When are you going to draw the line?"

Jay kept quiet for a long moment, and Grayson didn't prompt him to answer.

"It's the last time. I'm going to Milan, and we'll have it out. Everything."

"Good for you." Eriadne embodied a total bitch, and maybe, this time, Jay would open his eyes and see her for the spoiled slut she really was.

"Which is why I need to leave the firm in Robin's hands,"

Jay said.

Grayson groaned. He didn't bother to conceal the sound, certain Jay expected the reaction. "Robin Gallas is a wonderful investment specialist, but she's also a heart attack and a time bomb waiting to happen. You really think we can shove so much on her? I can watch the market and pull together all the reports, but someone in New York will have to make the deals."

"I have no other choice, Gray."

"I could come back—"

"No! End of discussion where that's concerned. You agreed to two weeks; you stay there for two weeks. After this period, I don't care what you do or how you screw yourself up. I'll know I did everything I could to get you on the right track again."

"And if I wanted to bring *you* back on the right track, I'd pull your head out of your ass and make you see how Eriadne Bellefort is nothing but a conniving, scheming witch who's never gonna let you go as long as you pant after her like a lovesick puppy."

When Jay didn't curse, Grayson's anger diffused. "Sorry."

"Okay."

His friend sounded oddly defeated, and he hated this impression even more than the hell-demon masquerading as an angel and playing with Jay's mind and heart.

"Go on ahead." Maybe the next few days would be make or break time for Jay. "I'll talk to Robin soon."

"Thanks, man."

About to cut the call, he paused in his step. The house had come into view, the back porch leading to the kitchen in plain sight. Inside the room, *she* hovered over her pots and pans and burning stoves. He'd sit at the pine table all day and watch her putter around in her crazy-loony, OCD-harried ways. And now that he thought of it, this morning, outside, Shayne had not struck him at all like a neurotic basket case. She'd smiled and laughed, and held her own against intimidating Mika. Hell, she'd even had the old codger wrapped around her little finger, for Mika had offered to saddle a horse for her. Something he never did. Except for Grayson's mother. *Don't go there,* he thought as the burn of forbidden pain flared up in his chest.

"Jay, listen, I just might be staying here a little longer than planned."

"How much longer?"

He could hear glee in the other man's voice, pictured the tall, buff Indo-Irish American sit up straighter in his seat.

Panic, unfamiliar and unexpected, swelled up and grabbed his throat in a stranglehold. He hadn't experienced such a debilitating attack in the past fourteen years, ever since he'd left. But he all too clearly remembered the feeling of helplessness that had crashed over him on a tidal wave when his mother had been sick.

What was he doing? Did he even have a clue?

From where he stood, he had an unobstructed view of the kitchen window opening onto the porch. Dawn had not yet pierced through the clouds, and with the light on in the room, the interior proved visible as if the sheer drapes didn't stand between the glass pane and Shayne, who stood at the sink. She talked with someone, hands sketching wide gestures to accentuate her point. Then she laughed. Shayne tipped her head back whenever she laughed, baring the long column of her graceful neck and exposing the dip of her throat.

His gut clenched, and the panic fled as fast as it had flitted in.

"I'm staying at least a few more weeks," he said into the phone.

He had agreed to teach Shayne how to ride. She'd confessed her green status as a rider, so he'd be looking at, at least, three to four weeks of daily lessons.

"Things so bad over there? I thought your aunt had the ranch running like well-tuned clockwork."

"She does."

Jay remained silent for a long beat. "The reason you're extending your stay; does she have a name?"

Grayson chuckled. Jay knew him well. Too soon to tell

anyone about Shayne, yet he couldn't keep the elation of a possible relationship to himself. He brimmed with the excitement, as bad as a teen with his first crush. "Shayne Morea."

"Indian?"

"British."

"Crikey," Jay joked with an exaggerated British accent. "Good for you, man. So I guess we won't be seeing you for a while?"

"Not unless Robin brings the whole place down in flames while you're gone. I trust you to rein the chaos in when you get back from Milan."

"Count on me," Jay promised. "And, Gray? Thanks, man."

"Anytime."

He cut the call and pocketed the cell. Without moving from his standpoint, he stared at the kitchen window and the woman standing there. As the sun slowly came out, the sheer curtains on the pane grew opaque, and when they turned the light off inside the room, he could no longer see the house's interior.

Could no longer see *her*....

And he craved to see her again. If he just had her within sight, everything in his messed-up life would fall into place, even if only for a moment.

What man dared hope deny such a strong pull, such an incapacitating need?

High time he gave in.

Chapter Six

*W*hat had possessed him to want to stay? Two weeks represented one thing; any more than this....

He had it bad for one woman. The decision happened in a split second, where he heard himself tell Jay he'd be here for longer than planned. Up until then, he hadn't contemplated the thought of sticking around. He didn't want to be here, in this place where remembrances of his parents, or his mother's illness, smacked him everywhere he glanced.

Until his gaze landed on Shayne, when he forgot everything else. Similar to an anchor, a life raft, in a stormy sea, she proved the one thing to keep him grounded.

How could she have this kind of profound effect on him barely two days after he'd met her?

Shayne made his stay bearable, and beyond a doubt, he needed her in his life for as long as he'd be here. She became his rock, indispensable to him.

He dwelled on this certitude the whole night, and at four the next morning, started toward the kitchen, where he'd find Shayne puttering away. He could hear the sizzle of frying fat, and smell the greasy, slight nauseous reek of hot vegetable oil the minute he reached the ground floor. How long had she been hard at work?

She'd come home late the previous night, having been out

all day and evening with Aurelie at Mrs. Harvey's bakery. His cousin mentioned something about shooting some recipe videos while there. Shayne had already gone up to her room by the time he cornered Aurelie in the hallway. He'd wanted to go see her but had restrained himself. What would he have told her? That he'd missed seeing her, missed spending time with her? Damn it, his behavior reeked of a lovesick fool's, or Jay panting after Eriadne. He'd sworn this would never happen to him, but look where he found himself today. At least, Shayne didn't seem a wicked hag like Eriadne; else, his judgment would be real flawed. Shayne didn't play games. At least, he hoped so.

He clutched the closed laptop under his arm as he trudged down the hallway toward the kitchen. In a few moments, he'd know for sure whether he and Shayne could have something, the hope akin to salvation for him as long as he remained with her, even if only for a few weeks. Or, else, whether he'd spend the next month desiring her from afar, with the need to have her, to be with her, eating his insides even more than the acid-burn of being back, while he told himself to stay away because she'd rejected him. He'd never lusted after a woman so much, never craved one with such overwhelming need. His focus had always been on other things. But back here in Freewill, his perspective changed. Life, and the future, no longer carried the frenetic pace of New York. Here, people lived for the moment, and he wanted his moment, and the next, to have Shayne in it, because to have her meant he could go on, that he didn't have to face the reality of the Warner heritage all around him.

On the threshold of the dining room, he paused. His heart hammered, the whoosh of blood at his temples loud, forcing him to concentrate on his purpose and not the overwhelming desire to turn tail and run. Everything inside him, at this precise moment, wanted to run away, but his instincts screamed for him to listen, to take a chance. The same certainty would grip him when he saw a last-minute-coup deal on the Forex market.

He had to trust himself.

Grayson entered the kitchen. Shayne had her back to him.

Today, she wore jeans and a pink, fitted blouse outlining her generous curves, her long, dark hair up in a tight bun, the golden line of her nape lay visible.

He could imagine the soft, downy hairs on her skin there, and how they'd feel against his lips if he went up to her and dropped a light kiss behind her ear, along her hairline.

His jeans grew tight, and he swallowed.

As if she felt him there, she turned, and the smile she gave him extended akin to an iron fist clamping on everything inside his ribcage. His head grew light, and he couldn't take in any air.

Damn, he had it bad.

"'Morning," she greeted in a singsong voice, before she returned her attention back to whatever lay in front of her.

"Hey."

Even as a teenager, he hadn't had time for girls. Not with his mother being so sick. He'd had girlfriends, and later, as a grown man, he'd had affairs. But the last time he remembered being tongue-tied around a girl was back in middle school, when he'd debated for weeks whether Annie Benton with the bubbly laugh and who sat next to him in math class would let him take her to the seventh-grade dance.

And he felt thirteen again. Awkward, gawky.

Shayne turned toward him, with a frown this time. "What's the matter?"

Could his turmoil be so obvious? The tension ate at him, similar to burning, corrosive acid. Time to jump in with the sharks of self-doubt and potential feminine rejection. "I need your advice, actually."

He strolled into the kitchen, to place the laptop on the table. The surface looked strangely uncluttered today; why wasn't Shayne cooking for a crowd that morning?

She ran the tap then walked toward him with a dishtowel in her grip, on which she wiped her hands.

"What is it?" she asked as she stopped next to him.

Soft heat radiated from her body, and in the cool early morning, he wanted to reach out and pull her to him. He wanted her warmth, to feel her in his arms. More, even. But he'd have to wait. A girl like Shayne deserved the whole nine yards in seduction and old-fashioned wooing before being roped into a scorching-hot affair. He'd take his time, focus his everything on the task of bowling her over. Damn if that wouldn't kill him, but he'd be patient, and win her little by little. After all, Shayne would be there for the next twelve weeks, at least. Ample time to make his move, in a slow and sure manner.

Grayson opened the laptop and turned it toward her. A swipe on the mouse's touch pad brought the screen to life. The page showed an e-commerce site, the search narrowed to three kinds of food processors. He pointed at the images.

"I need your professional opinion. Which one is best?"

Shayne squinted at the screen. "Why are you looking at that?"

"No specific reason." *Yeah, right!* "I just want to know which you think would be best."

"The second one. It's got more options, and the feeder and bowls allow for more volume. There's also better speed control on the device." She peered up at him. "I still have no clue what you need to know—"

He snaked a hand in front of her, and with his finger on the touch pad, tapped the mouse onto the Buy Now button. "Done."

"Wait a second." She straightened. "Did you just buy this food processor?"

"It should be here later today."

"But why? I really don't see you having to wield such a device in a kitchen—"

"Not me. You."

"I beg your pardon?"

"I got it for you."

Had it been a bad idea? Shayne should've jumped up with joy and thrown her arms around her neck, kissed him in thanks. Maybe not the last part; he got carried away imagining. But she shouldn't appear so shell-shocked, for sure.

"The old grinder you used blew a fuse, remember? You

needed a new one," he said.

"Yes, but...I would've managed. You didn't have to go and buy a new one." She gasped, and brought a hand up to cover her mouth. With a hard shove, she moved him from in front of the screen and peered at the buy confirmation page. "It cost nearly a thousand dollars."

"So?"

"Grayson!" She sighed. "It's a professional commercial kitchen food processor. You can make a kilogram of mayonnaise in a single go in the bowl."

"And that's not good?"

"Are you not hearing what I'm saying on purpose?"

She sounded angry. Not a good thing. She should've been happy. He'd gotten her the best equipment, according to her own opinion.

He moved to where she stood with her hands on the back of a chair, shoulders slumped. "Why are you taking this so hard? I thought you'd enjoy having some new equipment. It's no big deal."

She peeked up, eyes narrow. "No big deal? Are you bloody kidding me? A thousand dollars *is* a big deal."

"It cost less than a thousand."

"That is not the point!"

When she tried to move away, he reached out and clasped her shoulders. The rapid-fire words spewing out of her mouth died. Their eyes met, and even his words evaporated on his lips when he stared down into the deep darkness. He heard her hitch in a breath through her parted lips, and as he gazed at the soft, deep pink flesh, he wanted nothing else but to bow his head and touch his mouth to hers.

"It's a gift, Shayne."

"You shouldn't have—"

"There's only one thing you're allowed to say."

She blinked a few times. "Wh...what?"

He clasped her shoulders tighter and rubbed the pads of his thumbs along her collarbones. "'Thank you, Grayson.' That's all."

"But—"

"Shh. Say it. Just say what I want to hear, and we'll leave all of it behind us. We have to look forward, to the future."

Our future. He was jumping the gun.

Her dark gaze searched his, before she blinked and sank her teeth into her full lower lip.

His gut clenched, eager for his teeth to clamp onto that plump flesh as he took her mouth and made her his. He had to rein himself in, fast, otherwise he'd kiss her and she'd end up on the table, under him, her soft, warm body taking him in with the wild abandon he yearned for when he'd have her.

"Thank you, Grayson."

The words flowed from her lips, a gentle whisper to remind him she remained, at the heart of her, a delicate flower who needed careful handling.

Not for a horny cowboy to throw her on a kitchen table and have his way with her. Time he brought his self-control in. He'd be in Freewill for another month, at least. There'd be time to woo Shayne in the proper way.

With reluctance, he released her shoulders and took a step back. She batted her eyelids, surely unaware how much the movement made a man think of languorous bedroom eyes beckoning to come-hither. The breath hissed into his lungs as he forced himself to drag his gaze away from her face.

He turned toward the sink, and his gaze fell on the counter, onto a large dish full of what seemed to be yellow caviar. "What the heck is this?"

For a moment there, Shayne could've sworn he would kiss her. His eyes had grown dark, narrow, his jaw so tense a small muscle beat in one cheek. His beautiful mouth had pursed as if he were contemplating something...and she'd have bet her life on the surefire probability he would lower his head and kiss her.

Good thing she hadn't bet, because she'd be dead now. Without having felt his kiss.

Get a grip. She'd been furious with him, angered beyond reason at how he'd manipulated her and bought the humongous food processor. That thing belonged in a restaurant kitchen, not a family ranch. And blast if the device wouldn't feed her inability to cook for less than ten people at a time. She didn't need further encouragement to whip out food to feed a regiment every single day.

But one look from him, one touch of his warm hands on her shoulders, and her anger had melted faster than ghee in a hot pot. Worse, the emotion had flash-burned quicker than butter turned brown in a too-hot pan. Her fury had sizzled, scorched, and evaporated the second she peered into those chocolate-colored eyes. When he'd opened his mouth and beckoned her to say what he wanted her to say, she'd had absolutely no desire to offer any resistance, and from afar, had heard herself say the words, breathless and husky, her voice all but begging him to take her, to have his way with her.

Could she be so much of a shameless hussy?

"Shayne?" he called out. "What are you doing with this caviar thing? I didn't know yellow caviar even existed."

"It's not caviar, silly." Food. Back on her territory. Staring at the confusion on his face, her confidence shot up, and she laughed.

She went to the sink, where she washed her hands, before she moved to his side. "It's called *boondi*. I'm going to make *laddoos* with it. I'll be teaching the folks at the bakery how to make this today, and I thought they'd want to taste the food first so they know what they'll be making."

"Okay. Translation, please?"

Shayne threw her head back and laughed. She started pointing at the bowl on the counter, next to the frying pan half-full of hot oil. "You start by making a paste of gram flour with a little plain flour. Just add water until it's a thick consistency. Then, over the hot oil, you take a rice strainer"— she picked up the flat ladle with the many small holes— "and you strain the paste through the holes. The batter ends up as small droplets in the oil, which you remove when fried and dunk in heavy syrup. You let them soak, and you get *boondi*, what you see here."

"The caviar."

"It's nothing like caviar. Caviar is disgusting."

"You don't like it?"

"No. And it's way too salty."

"Says the one who probably strives on Indian food. Why are curries always so salty? I end up downing a jug of beer after every plate and still wake up the next morning as dehydrated as if I were hungover."

"Indian cooks are liberal with the salt, because in India, they love their condiments. I never use too much in my curries."

"I wouldn't know, since I haven't tasted your curries," Grayson said softly.

Was he taking the mickey out of her?

Or, worse, could he be serious?

Her lips parted and she sucked in a breath. He was serious. "You...you tasted my *pani puri*."

"Only one, because Aurelie had polished the rest off by the time I got back in." He paused, eyes narrowed and intense. "And I had other things on my mind when I ate your *puri*."

Like the fact he had licked her fingers in the process? Heat flared up all over her body as she recalled the warm rasp of his tongue against her skin, the moist softness of his lips as they had closed on her fingers.

Stop looking at me like this, she wanted to hurl. But the words remained stuck in her throat.

"I...I better get back to work." She forced herself to look the other way.

"Doing what?"

He stood so close; his breath caressed the side of her neck, and she tamped down the shiver coursing through her. He shouldn't see the effect he had on her. More so because she was an idiot falling for the pretty face of a man who had no desire to seduce her.

Because if he did, she should've been flat on her back on the table behind them, without any need for her to urge him to do wicked things to her as he'd already be one step ahead in the ravishment game.

Oh no, she wouldn't make the mistake of tumbling into a man's bed before she knew if he'd prove an arse or not. The debacle with Pratik had taught her so much, if anything else. Friends with benefits implied something obvious—*friends*. People who knew each other.

"I need to make the *laddoos*," she stated.

Shayne risked a glance to the side when he remained silent. He'd propped a hip against the counter and stood with his arms crossed, his eyes on her.

"Show me," he said.

Had he hypnotized her? With every word pouring from his lips, his power over her grew, until every cell inside her screamed to do his bidding all while she should be telling him to get lost. Where was the real Shayne, the tough girl who'd never let herself be bullied by the idiots at school and on the local football team?

She should get on with her work, and who cared if he watched?

She dipped her hands in a bowl of fresh water, and, with the tips of her fingers, raked a small amount of *boondi* into her hand. Rolling the squishy droplets of fried, syrupy dough into her palm, she formed a compact ball, which she placed on an empty plate. She then added the final touch, a sliver of almond pressed into the *laddoo*.

"Doesn't look hard," Grayson said.

"You want to try?"

She bit her tongue as soon as the invitation left her lips. What had gotten into her? She should get rid of him as quickly as possible.

Please, make him squeamish, so he'll bail out.

"I'd love to," he replied.

Bloody hell!

Okay, she just had to treat him as she would a trainee in her kitchen, a student. Be professional, detached, aloof. "Wash your hands first."

He went to the tap, rinsed his hands, and when he reached for the dishtowel she'd abandoned on the edge, she spoke.

"Keep your hands wet. You'll need the moisture so the *boondi* won't stick."

Step by step, she took him through the process of rolling *laddoos*. But Grayson wasn't used to manipulating Indian sweets, and what seemed to her an obvious task proved a skill he hadn't mastered.

"No, not like this," she said on a chuckle when he closed his fist so hard the yellow droplets squished between his fingers. "Slowly. Take your time."

And, since every cook and culinary school student knew techniques were best shown than explained, she fell onto instinct. She found herself holding the back of his right hand in the cradle of her palm, with her fingers closing over his to demonstrate how to roll the sweets.

She could swear a zap of electricity shot up her arm where she touched him, and based on the way he brought his head up sharply to stare at her, he must've felt it, too.

Their eyes met, hands stilled, and her breath locked itself somewhere between her lungs and her lips.

Goodness, he would kiss her. He had to.

As if in slow motion, he lowered his head. Shayne parted her lips, eager for the touch of his mouth against hers, yearning for the zing of pleasure to course through her when he made contact—

The sound of bhangra drums screeched into the kitchen, and she jumped with the surprise. A small yelp also escaped her, drowned under the ruckus of the music. Bloody Dave. It had to be her brother calling. His timing sucked.

She risked a glance at Grayson; he appeared unfazed by the near-missed kiss, as well as the cacophony of the music. The song had sounded so joyful and boisterous when she first heard it. Who would've thought it would make such a lousy ringtone?

Every time her phone belted out the tune, she almost jumped out of her skin and had to calm her racing heart.

Why did Grayson appear so unaffected, though? "Most non-Indian people clutch their ears when they hear bhangra drums."

He laughed. "Believe me, the first few times I heard the tune, my brain would screech to a halt. But Karryn, Jay's sister, used to play the song so much when at his place it became background noise after a while."

The phone still rang. Shayne cursed under her breath and ran the tap to wash the sticky syrup from her hands. She quickly dried her hands, and picked up the cell. Indeed, Dave calling.

"Wot?" she threw in greeting, her accent thickening with her irritation. He better have a good reason to be reaching out, when she'd already told him to get off her back.

"What are you doing there, Shayne? Trying to become the female version of potty-mouthed Chef Ramsay?"

"What are you talking about?"

"You don't know?" His voice grew louder. "You really have no clue?"

"Of course I don't, you git. Do I usually play dumb?"

"Shayne, what are you doing? If Mum finds this...."

"If Mum finds what?" A headache started to build behind her forehead. What had she done so dire?

"Thank God I had set up a Google alert for you. The minute your name came up, I received a notification."

"Fuck you. A notification about what? Don't make me have to worm it out of you, Dave."

"Do you have Internet access there right now?"

She glanced at the laptop Grayson had brought in with him. Stalking to the machine, she flipped the lid open and tapped the mouse pad to open an Internet browser window. "What am I looking for?"

"You really have no clue—"

"If I had a bloody fucking clue, I wouldn't be asking, would I, Dave?"

"Gosh, no need to get your knickers in a twist—"

"Oh, that's rich, coming from the man who just asked me if I had all my marbles straight," she bit out. "What's the facking address?"

"YouTube."

Dread, thick and dense, akin to solidifying cement, pooled into her stomach. It could not be....

"Type your name in the search bar, and watch the videos coming up."

"I'll get back to you." Dave protested, but she cut him off in midsentence and set the phone on silent so she wouldn't have to hear him calling back.

She had more important things to do.

"What's wrong?" Grayson asked as he stopped next to her.

Oh no. She'd forgotten about him. She couldn't let him see this. Whatever "this" turned out to be. Could Pratik, or any one of her ex-boyfriends, have shot a video of her and uploaded it? Did the world know she had a sex tape online when she herself didn't have any clue?

The search page on YouTube came up.

Shayne only needed to see the thumbnails from the three uploaded videos to know they weren't sex tapes.

No, they were worse, as in, the videos she and Aurelie had made the previous day at the bakery. The same ones where, alone in the kitchen, they had fallen back on their trading-insults-type of banter. She'd called Aurelie all sorts of names, chastised the girl for being such an incompetent idiot in the kitchen. Aurelie had not let her off the hook either; Shayne had borne her fair share of insults, but the world had heard her being a spiteful cow.

She didn't need much more to ignite the anger smoldering inside her—first, because of Aurelie's hiding of the truth and luring her here under false pretenses; second, of Grayson's high-handed manner of buying her the food processor.

And third, the debilitating attraction she felt for him. The man made a mess out of her.

To know she had a very legitimate outlet for all her rage

powered her.

She slammed the laptop closed and stormed out of the kitchen toward the basement door. She'd find the deceitful, conniving little bitch there.

Grayson followed hot on her heels, but she paid him no heed.

"Shayne, what's the matter?"

"Your bloody cousin. She's the problem." She pulled the basement door open and stumbled back when the vibration from the noise of a virtual bomb explosion slammed into her. Her back landed smack against Grayson's chest, and he grabbed her to keep her from falling.

Too incensed to reckon he was touching her again, she shrugged him off and stormed down the stairs.

Aurelie held a remote she wielded like a sword. On the screen, the character of Vanorra carried out the same moves and dispatched a swarm of zombies with a single, neat strike.

Shayne wouldn't dispatch the devious git before her with a clean strike. No, she'd make Aurelie pay.

"Turn that thing off, or I will," she shouted, to be heard above the noise.

Aurelie rolled her eyes and pressed a button on her remote; the image on the screen stilled and silence flooded the room. "What's gotten into you? Are you PMSing?"

"How could you do this to me?" With a pointed finger, she poked at her friend's shoulder.

"Ouch, that hurts." Aurelie slapped her finger away.

"I should do more than hurt you, you crazy bitch, after the latest stunt you've pulled."

"What stunt?"

"The bloody videos. You uploaded them!"

"Of course I did."

"But these weren't the actual videos we were supposed to shoot. We didn't even have a demonstration in there." She paused. "Unless someone wanted to learn how to curse like a Briton from Southall."

The fire of her anger left her and her shoulders slumped. Everything went from bad to dire. Every single moment since she'd stepped into Freewill had gone wrong. Had her mother cursed her escape from London? "I should get out of here."

She turned, to stop in her tracks when she came up against Grayson's T-shirt-covered chest.

Grayson. She'd have loved to get to know him. Impossible. She had to get away, excuse herself with Mrs. Harvey and the other folks at the bakery, and head back to London. What had gotten into her to think she could strike out on her own and make it through? She'd throw herself on Aunt Shilpa's mercy and beg to have her job at *Kadai Haveli* back.

But first, she had to make Aurelie delete the videos from the site. Dave had found them because he'd had a Google alert set to her name. No one else knew her, though, so she doubted other people had come across the videos. She could still recover and clear her reputation before any lasting damage got done.

"Where are you going?" Aurelie asked.

"Home," Shayne murmured.

"But you can't. We just started the vlog—"

She whirled to face the other woman. "*You* started the vlog and made a farce out of it. Not only does the kitchen resemble a war zone on there, we do nothing but insult one another the whole time. What were you thinking?"

Aurelie waved her words away with her free hand. "I know what I'm doing."

"Do you?"

"Girls—" Grayson started, but they both turned hard, narrowed stares onto him and he clammed up.

"Have you even seen the page?" Aurelie asked.

"I saw what I had to."

"Which means you jumped to conclusions."

Shayne snorted.

Aurelie turned to the open laptop on the floor. With a little drumming on the keyboard, she brought the YouTube page to display on the blown-up screen.

"What are you doing?" Shayne asked. "I have no intention of watching that."

"Shut up, and look at the cursor," Aurelie snapped. "See how many views we've had?"

"Twenty-three thousand, and climbing." Grayson whistled. "How long has the clip been up?"

"Less than twelve hours," Aurelie confirmed.

Shayne traveled her gaze from one cousin to the other. "What does it mean?"

"It means many people have found the video and watched it."

Bloody hell. "You've got to be kidding me." So many people had heard her being a sad, sour, and disgruntled bitch? "You have to take them down."

"Are you out of your mind? We've just found ourselves a niche there."

"These are not even cooking-demonstration videos—"

"And everyone who uploads video recipes puts up a demonstration vid," Aurelie cut in. "People are tired of that. They want something different."

"They want to see the cooks swearing at one another?"

"People want to see reality, real people. Why do you think *Jersey Shore* is so popular?"

"For God's sake, the only thing more real than *Jersey Shore* is *TOWIE*. We're nothing more than a facking joke there!"

"What's *TOWIE*?" Grayson asked.

Too tired to keep on arguing, she replied him. "*The Only Way Is Essex*. The acronym makes *TOWIE*. British reality show."

"I suppose you haven't read the comments," Aurelie said.

"Telling us we're a bunch of foulmouthed bitches with nothing better to do than waste our time and that of the viewers?"

"No, stupid. People actually love what we're doing. See, look at the comment from some pauldanes1978 here. 'You girls sound so real, it's almost too good to be true.'"

"He must be fluent in sarcasm," Shayne threw out.

Aurelie rolled her eyes. "Cindy66 says, 'That's the wackiest video I've seen about Indian food. And I loved your recipe, made it without any glitch. Keep it up!'"

"She must be delusional."

"Amrita_Sita54, who is from India, by the way. 'Very good *barfi* recipe. I never knew the trick about having a few spoonfuls of water at the bottom of the pan when boiling milk. For the first time in thirty years, I haven't burned the milk when making sweets. Thank you.'"

At this one, Shayne remained silent. Could the woman really mean what she'd written?

"We're on to something here, Shayne."

"I don't know."

Things were going too far, too fast. She had to pause, gather her thoughts, in order to make some sense of what just happened.

So she turned toward the stairs and started back up.

"Where are you going?" both Grayson and Aurelie asked.

"I need to think," she threw over her shoulder. Once upstairs in the hallway, she didn't bother to close the door and traipsed out to the back porch, where she fell in a heap on the puffy cushions on the swing. The big red roses on the pale cream background of the worn fabric seemed to wrap themselves around her, offering the solace she craved.

She forced her mind to go blank. Too much rolled and ebbed in her head. She closed her eyes and focused on her breathing, one of the meditation techniques her mother had tried to get her into. Not that Anjali Morea practiced what she preached. Shayne's mum reminded her of a hot pressure cooker with a faulty pressure valve, always on the verge of bursting with tension.

She jumped when something warm settled on her shoulders. Eyes wide open, she peered up at Grayson, who draped a light blanket over her.

"You'll catch your death from the morning cold out here," he said in his soft, soothing voice.

He'd pulled on a jacket, the one with the hoodie he'd worn the other day.

Realizing how cold she'd grown when the blanket radiated gentle warmth into her body, she shivered and pulled the tasseled edges closer across her chest. "Thanks."

He sat down next to her. The swing moved. Afraid she'd tumble down head first, seeing as she'd pulled her legs under her, her worries abated when he stilled the movement with a booted foot on the floor.

He must be used to this swing, know every rock and ebb from it.

"What's the matter, Shayne?"

She stared out toward the horizon, where a fine line of light spread left and right. "Those videos weren't meant to go up."

"I would suppose so. Neither you nor my cousin had any holds barred on there."

She snorted, to which he laughed.

"Answer me truthfully. What's the real problem?"

Should she tell him? The emotions roiled inside of her, a harsh turmoil to sicken her stomach and stiffen her muscles. All her life, she had striven to be proper, polite, what her mother and their society expected of her. Behind closed doors, she let loose, but in public, she kept her honor and the family's intact.

Grayson drew closer. He reached out and settled his thumb and forefinger onto her chin and made her turn toward him.

His eyes were serious and intense, jaw strong and clamped with tension. Something else hovered on his features. Worry.

For her?

Staring at him like this, with his caring gaze on her, she wanted no secrets between them, nothing but trust and the ability to lean onto each other for the support both knew they'd give without any condition attached.

So she took a deep breath and started talking. "On those videos, it's not me."

"What do you mean?"

111

"It's me, but not." At the confusion on his face, she sighed. Sitting up straighter, she sent the swing rocking again. She shot a hand out to grab the porch's railing before she fell, but Grayson stilled the movement with his foot once again.

"Why don't you tell me exactly what you meant to say?" he coaxed.

"I know you've heard me swear and curse. You've seen me at my worse. And yes, I do have a potty mouth. But I never do so in public. I behave properly around people, in general. I don't give my family any reason to be ashamed of me." She paused. "But the world is going to see me belting out curse after curse. Hell, even Gordon Ramsay sounds like a choirboy compared to me."

"And you're afraid your family is going to see it?"

She nodded.

"So, if I've got this straight, you're the real you in private. But in public, you put on a different persona."

Shayne shrugged, not knowing how else to say.

He seemed to ponder her reply, brows furrowed, before he broke the silence.

"Isn't it tiring?"

Not what she'd expected to hear. And frankly, what did she think he would say? No one had ever asked her that question, either. The words tumbled from her mouth. "It is."

"Don't you think it's better for everyone to see you for who you really are?" He paused. "No one can hold two faces up without breaking down sometime."

"I know, but...."

"But what?"

He reached out, and when he brushed his fingers against her temple to tuck away the lock of hair that had broken from her bun, she stifled a moan. His touch came at her light, delicate, and a small tremor of pleasure and anticipation charged through her blood from the point of contact.

Once he'd settled the lock behind her ear, he didn't pull back. Instead, he kept playing with strands from the long fringe she usually tied back with clips.

Words bubbled up in her throat to die on the cusp of her lips at his continuous attention.

"Who is the real Shayne?"

Against her will, she grinned when she pondered the reply. "The potty mouth."

He smiled, too. Bloody hell, he had a gorgeous smile.

"Is she a bad person, the potty mouth?"

She shook her head.

"Then why are you afraid to let her out? We are who we are, Shayne. The sooner we face and accept it, the better."

Who are you, *and have* you *accepted who you are?*

"Show the world who you truly are. I'm sure everyone will be dazzled."

"If they don't die of shock first."

"They won't. Trust me."

She should, shouldn't she? Everything inside her strove to believe him, to trust him, as he asked. But that proved..."Scary."

"No one said it would be easy."

True. She wasn't thinking of "coming out" as the potty mouth, though. No, her thoughts focused on Grayson, on her, on them....

"You know what? I prefer to think of anything else but that right now," she confessed.

He dropped his hand; she wanted to grab his palm and urge him to keep on playing with her hair. She culled the desire before she did anything stupid. Such as pulling his hand back, and placing it directly onto her skin. Goodness, she craved his touch—

Grayson laughed, and she lost all her train of thought at the twinkle in his eye.

"I know exactly how to take your mind off everything, sweetheart."

Chapter Seven

$\mathcal{A}$ few moments later, Shayne dragged in a breath as she approached the wide enclosure fenced by thick logs. Grayson walked behind her, making her hyperaware of his presence shadowing her this way. The sliver of apprehension refused to leave her, though, no matter how hot and bothered he made her feel.

"When you mentioned you'd take my mind off my problems," she said, "I imagined something else."

Such as, a kiss, or a tumble into warm sheets. Definitely not *that*. She gulped, and her stomach cramped with unease and tension. Bloody hell, she couldn't do it.

He stopped a few inches from her, his body heat radiating to hers and calling to her lust and hormones like a magnet to iron. With her hair up in its bun, his warm breath feathered across her nape. Shivers traveled down her body, replacing the dread with a different kind of coiled tension. How she wanted to take a step back and burrow against his broad chest. But panic kept her frozen, and instead, she turned to stare into his face.

Grayson smiled a beautiful, cheeky grin to make his eyes sparkle with mischief. Blast. Why couldn't what he'd planned involve him, and, as she turned toward the fenced corral, not *that*?

"You didn't get a clue when I asked you to change your

shoes for Aunt Tracy's riding boots?"

"I thought you wanted us to go for a walk, for which I'd need sturdy footwear. Not...." She paused, and shuddered. "*This.*"

He opened the corral's gate and grabbed her hand, to haul her into the wide oval space. "*This* has a name; it's Bella."

Shayne's fingers remained stiff and try as she wanted to curl her hand around his and never let go, she couldn't move beyond the dread making her heart hammer. Grayson pulled her toward the horse and made her stop next to it.

"That thing is taller than I am."

How did he, and anyone else, ever hope she could get on the animal and let it take her anywhere? The beast towered above her, and stank, the smell almost as bad as stepping into the back of her butcher's shop in Southall, all animal and flesh, reeking and pungent. She sucked in a deep breath through her mouth, to keep the smells at bay.

"Bad idea. I better go back—"

"You're not a quitter."

Grayson's voice rang loud and strong, thrumming with conviction. The certainty in his tone stopped the words on her lips. She stared into his too-handsome and too-serious face. What she saw made her take another step back. He had faith in her.

When he placed his hand on her shoulder, she leaned into his touch.

"I'm totally a coward, though," she admitted.

"No, you're not."

He released her shoulder, to travel his hand to her cheek, which he cupped in his palm. Heat flooded her at his touch, liquefied her whole body, and she parted her lips while her eyes sought his. His gaze had darkened and appeared dangerous. Inviting, like only sin could beckon.

Shayne wanted to draw closer; he would bridge the rest of the distance until their lips would touch. How many times would she yearn for this man to kiss her? And when would he bloody take her, once and for all, and put an end to her misery?

He rubbed the pad of his thumb on her cheekbone. "I promised I'd make a Midwest cowgirl out of you."

Then he drew away.

What? She yearned to hurl the question at him, ask him what in heaven's name he thought he played at with her.

She jumped when the horse bumped its warm nose against her shoulder. The creature gave a soft whinny, reminding her of a chuckle. A yelp escaped Shayne when the horse tried to poke her again with its muzzle, and her fear turned to abject fury when Grayson laughed.

At her.

She balled her hand into a fist and thumped her arm against his stomach. A small measure of satisfaction danced through her when he let out a shocked breath.

"No need to be so angry, sweetheart."

"Don't you dare laugh at me."

"Okay, I won't. Promise."

Why did she feel he would only bide his time before he could make fun of her again?

"Let's get on with your first lesson," he added.

She glanced at the horse, standing next to them. "I really don't think it's a good idea."

"Buck up, Shayne. You're gonna do this, and I'm sure you'll be great."

"The horse is scary."

"No, she isn't. Bella is what we call a babysitter. All the kids on the ranch learn to ride on her. She's very patient."

"I weigh a lot more than a kid. Won't she mind?"

Bad thing to have said, because she could feel Grayson's gaze traveling all over her body. Slowly, with languid ease. Blast him, he made her feel hot and sexy at the same time she wondered why she couldn't be slimmer and more toned. Desire warred with apprehension—the perfect deadly cocktail to shoot her nerves into incompetence.

"First things first," he started. "Always approach a horse from the front, or the side. The more the animal can see you approaching, the better. You should never come from behind it, got it?"

She nodded.

"Later, I'll show you how to groom and tack up a horse. You should do that before taking it out of the stable. Now, prior to getting on, one thing you always have to check is the cinch, or the girth as it's called on an English saddle." He patted Bella's side. "This is an English saddle, by the way. We all learn the English way before moving to a Western saddle, tradition of show-jumping champions and all that going on here."

He shifted his touch to the horse's belly, where he pushed two fingers between the animal's side and the strap there. "See? It should be neither too tight nor too loose. Just enough for two fingers to slide in."

Shayne's heart still hammered, but she tried to make sense of his instructions. So far, what he'd said reminded her of the *mise en place* before starting any recipe, when she pulled out all the ingredients and utensils she would need and arranged them on the workstation.

"Come on. I'll help you get on."

She ran the tip of her tongue against her dry lips. "I...am not sure I really want to."

"Shayne," he growled.

At the hint of annoyance in his voice, and the way his face grew serious, she shouldn't goad him. She had no way out here. Maybe if she showed him how bad a rider she'd be, he'd get off her back. Grayson Warner would never be convinced of anything without seeing it with his own two eyes; she was certain of it.

"Fine," she bit out. "Let's do this."

"Just how familiar are you exactly with horses?" he asked as he shook his head.

"I've read *Black Beauty*. And Jilly Cooper's *Riders*. Though I skimmed the book more to get to the parts Rupert Campbell-Black featured in, but—" She stopped rambling. "I've never even gotten so close to one before."

"First time for everything."

The words were so soft she wondered if she'd heard him. "Not for everything. I mean, look at adultery or violence. There should never be a first time for these. Don't you agree? There cannot be a first time for just about everything—"

Only when he grabbed her arm and tugged her back to the horse's side did she realize she'd taken backward steps during her spiel.

"Are you trying to drown a fish or something here?" he asked. "You *are* taking your first riding lesson today, even if I have to put you on the horse myself."

"I'm too heavy for you," she retorted, trying her best to forget the insistent, commanding note in his voice urging her to do his bidding.

That, and the insane compulsion inside her to do everything he asked. Bloody hell, she never became a doormat, or a woman a man could spin around to whatever tune he played. What the hell happened to her?

You're in love, a little voice whispered in her head.

Get out of here—

Shayne froze. How could she love Grayson, after knowing him for less than four days?

And yet, how could she *not* be in love with him, when four days proved enough to show her who he really was, and how he'd cared for her when her nose had started to bleed? No one had ever looked after her the way he had....

She'd fallen for only this much so quickly? *Blast!*

"You wanna try me, Shayne?"

Out here, in the open Wyoming plains, Grayson Warner became every inch the Midwest cowboy. Even his voice had changed. He no longer spoke with the deep rumble of New York's accent, instead falling back into a lazier, smoother drawl.

And glancing up into his eyes, she found the edge of danger again. Not cutthroat as what one would expect to see in the gaze of a Wall Street shark, but a more elemental, primeval danger speaking of the earth, of mankind, and of what men and women had been put on the planet to do.

"I'm not playing you," she mumbled.

He gazed at her for what seemed to her an eternity. "Good. I don't like players."

The question hovered on the tip of her tongue, and she wondered whether she should ask it, or better yet, to let it drop. Neither one of them needed to add oil to the raging fire that burned between them.

But like every cook knew, some things did taste better when flambéed.

"What do you like?" she asked softly.

Did she imagine it, or did his nostrils flare? He took a step forward, until he loomed over her. She'd never bothered with the difference in their heights before, but as she glanced up, all the way from his strong, T-shirt-clad chest under the opened hoodie, along his throat and wide neck, to his clenched jaw and the tight-slashed mouth, she reckoned he had to stand close to a foot taller than she.

A small muscle throbbed in his cheek, his eyes narrow and hooded. The rim of his cowboy hat threw shadows on the upper part of his face, making him appear even more lethal.

Time stood still while they stared at one another.

Then he broke the silence.

"I like you," he murmured.

She closed her eyes at the confession. The answer to all the prayers she didn't know she'd sent out until now. He liked her. While she'd fallen in love with him.... And in a predicament, because he would leave soon. Hell, *she* was leaving the US in a few weeks. Where would that make them end up, if ever there happened to be any them—

All the thoughts in her mind scrambled as she felt him draw nearer, as if having eyes closed amplified all her other senses. His body heat radiated out to her, and she leaned toward him like a flower searching for the sun. His warm breath tickled the skin between her nose and her mouth; she smiled at the feeling, still smiling when he pressed his lips to hers.

Gentle, hot, yielding. His mouth characterized everything she'd imagined it to be, and more. He coaxed her into an exchange of playful kisses. A laugh bubbled in her throat at his relentless teasing, and when she parted her lips to let the sound out, he pressed closer and swiped the tip of his tongue along her lower lip.

Shayne gasped, which allowed him to push his tongue farther into her mouth, and engage hers into sensuous play.

A kiss like this had to be accompanied by full-body contact. To hell with propriety and decorum. She wanted him, and she'd take what she wanted. Especially when he seemed to so gladly offer. *Live for the moment.* It's what she'd always done, the only way she knew how to live.

So she snaked her arms up his chest and shoulders until she could twine them behind his neck. She took a step forward, into the last breadth of distance between them, and molded her body to his.

His groan reverberated against her mouth, and he wrapped his arms around her and crushed her even more to the hard length of his taut, masculine body.

With not a millimeter of space between them, Grayson deepened the kiss. He plundered her mouth, and she gave herself up to him. He tasted foreign, totally unknown, but male and potent and singeing hot. They hungrily danced their tongue against the other's, while trying their best not to let the kiss end. As if they couldn't get enough of the other's lips, desperation coursed through the exchange and made them cling to one another. Like their life depended on it.

Grayson's arms around her loosened. She moaned at the lost contact, and felt him smile against her mouth.

A wisp of cold air danced along the small of her back, replaced a second later by the warm touch of big, male hands he'd snuggled under her blouse. The heat from his skin shocked her, made her press herself tighter against him.

He rubbed his thumbs against her skin, in small, lazy moves that made her shiver and turned her knees to jelly. Blast him.

She needed a breath, needed air, in order to steel her body against the assault of his touch on her skin.

With reluctance, she broke the kiss, to gulp in a huge inhale. Leaning as she did into him, her forehead pressed against the side of his neck. She exhaled, slowly, against his skin, and his touch on her stilled.

The roar of her heated blood in her ears grew hushed, until she could make out the sounds of the ranch all around them. The horse snorted and clopped a hoof on the ground, and in the distance, she thought she heard men call out to each other.

Yet, in Grayson's arms, where she still remained ensconced, nothing of all that permeated. She wanted nothing else but to stay there and let everything drift away into oblivion.

She craved to have Grayson make love to her. If his kiss could scorch the living daylights out of her, what would his touch, and his lovemaking, inject into her? Delicious death and rebirth?

He'd kissed her, yes, but did it mean he wanted anything more with her? Shayne didn't dare open her eyes to look up, in case she'd see regret on his features, in case he averted his gaze from hers. She couldn't tolerate it if he did so.

She stiffened, and Grayson, too, grew tense.

At a loss, Shayne drew away from his arms while keeping her eyes lowered.

"I...you should get me on the horse," she muttered as she stared at the ground.

"Good idea."

And just like that, he dashed all her hopes of their one perfect kiss ever developing into something more.

ᗢ

It's been a week. Grayson leaned against the corral's fence late one afternoon. *A fucking week.*

Shayne hadn't spoken to him in that long, ever since the kiss on the day of her first riding lesson. She met with him every morning for the sessions, but damn if she went beyond the obvious chitchat and asking him to clue her in about her riding technique. She'd then leave the stable before he could get a chance to talk to her, spending her days at the bakery.

And when she came back to the ranch, Marion Gilmore would rope her into training her for soccer.

He watched Shayne and Marion, as well as a handful of other girls from the town, getting on with the five-a-side soccer match in the field beyond the corral. Shayne appeared light on her feet, and she flittered all over her side of the field with sharp speed. Once she had the ball between her feet, no player could dream of winning it back from her. The only one who could stop her progress became the goalkeeper, a girl with phenomenal bouncing energy and who reminded him of a haywire pinball while she guarded the goal.

Shouts and hollers resounded, and he spied the group of ranch hands cheering on the game from the edges of the field.

"You're not turning into a pervert, are you, Gray?" Jed stopped next to him and leaned on the fence.

"What the hell are you talking about?"

Jed nodded toward the soccer game. "May I remind you these girls are all of ten or eleven? You've been watching them like a lion stalking its prey for the past six days."

"Get your fucked-up mind out of the gutter, you sick fuck! Why would I be looking at kids?"

"I'm the father of three girls, Gray. I do what I have to do."

He shivered. He could understand where Jed came from, but to think he looked at kids? "That is just sick, you know it, for you to accuse me—"

"I'm not accusing you."

"Fucking right you're not! I wonder what it'd be like if you were slinging charges at me."

"I wouldn't be slinging charges, man. There wouldn't be a tooth left in your mouth if I had beef with you."

Damn it, could this be the same skinny geek who'd hidden in lockers at school? He didn't want any beef with Jed, and the man was only looking after his own. Hell, if he'd had kids, he would've protected them with his life and everything else. Kept them in a protective bubble and never let them out. The kind of insulated existence living on a ranch like Heart's Anchor could provide. Big cities like New York were no place to bring kids up. If he ever had any children, he'd raise them here.

He lurched forward as the realization slammed into him. *You don't want to be here, remember?* Yes, he did recall the little fact, but now that he came here, his perspective shifted. The more he stayed on the ranch, the more the certainty imbued in him he was nothing like his father. And even if he did have shades of Bobby Warner in him, he could, and would, do anything in his power to not mess up like his old man had.

Maybe he hadn't wanted to come back because he would have to accept this fact about him. How he held a Midwest country boy in him, his life and values here, and chasing after a fortune and the Forex market back in New York proved nothing but a smokescreen to keep him from having to face the real truth.

He *was* Grayson Warner of Freewill, with the blood of his ancestors, the founders of this estate, flowing in his veins. Blood that heard the call of *his* land when he stood on it.

"You look a little green," Jed said.

Grayson snapped out of his thoughts.

In four days, he could get out of here and head back to New York. The original plan. Jay had imposed the two-week exile on him. Nothing more. Thanks to Shayne's presence at Heart's Anchor, the days had passed in a blur. She helped him forget where he stood. And thanks to Jay being away in Milan, he spent most of his time on the computer, stalking the Forex market because he shadowed Robin who found herself alone in the New York office.

Time slipped by, and he'd done a good job of blanking out his surroundings.

Except that the place had worked on him. Without conscious thinking, his instincts ran in the background to breathe the force of the land back into his soul—the very thing he'd dreaded ever since he'd left here.

Fourteen years ago, the blow of his father's immaturity and the price they'd all had to pay had weighed him down and clouded his judgment. Over the years, the nameless dread snowballed, until it filled him up completely. Grayson only thought of how he'd carried his father's DNA in his genetic makeup. Nothing else.

It took coming back here, onto his land, into his world, to know he'd been wrong.

He was a Warner, and not a fuck-up like his father.

He still had a long way to go toward becoming who he had to be, the man the ranch demanded he be. But the right track beckoned.

The memory of the kiss he'd shared with Shayne scorched through him. Large parts of his heart had expanded with the realization he didn't represent the destructive force his father had been. To know he'd found his place, come where he was meant to be all along, made his whole heart swell when he thought of her.

With the sweet taste of her lips in his mind, and the remembrance of her lush curves pressed to his frame, he was complete. Finally. A sense of peace, foreign and utterly unexpected, descended on him, washing down all the way through his soul and into his gut.

He needed Shayne.

If only she'd have him, though....

He forced his gaze to land on her, where she ran a few hundred yards away. So short she barely stood a head taller than the Freewill tweens, she did stand out of the crowd.

"Earth to Grayson." Jed waved a hand in front of his eyes. "What you staring at with such a fierce glare?"

"I'm not glaring," he growled.

"Sure you are." Jed pulled himself up to stand straighter. "Okay, I get it. Man, she is stacked!"

"Speak of her in the same manner once more and we'll see

whose teeth fly out first," Grayson bit out.

"You're toast."

Damn right. And the unnerving woman wouldn't even talk to him.

Jed laughed. "Now that I know you've got it bad for a legal chick, I'll let you off the hook. She sounds like a little hellcat, though." He thumped Grayson on the shoulder. "You're gonna have your hands full. But you know what? They're worth it," he added with a wink, before he left.

Grayson trained his eyes from his friend's departing form and back onto Shayne. As if she'd felt his gaze on her, she glanced up, and stopped dead in her tracks on the field. From this distance, he couldn't see all the nuances of emotion that must be passing on her face.

She seemed to notice the ball flying in her direction. With a quick jump, she bounced the ball off her chest and chased down the field again.

What must she have been thinking? And how in heaven's name did he get her to talk to him?

How did he get her to stay?

Whoa there! Surely he was jumping the gun? He might've come to the conclusion he wanted to have lots more to do with his ranch, but he hadn't thought about the future, about his day-to-day life, yet.

As if summoned, the life he'd left behind only eleven days ago made its existence known in the vibration against his thigh, where he'd placed his BlackBerry in his jeans pocket.

The screen displayed the alert for an email marked urgent. He clicked the buttons, accessed the blank message from Robin carrying a .jpg attachment. Grayson clicked the link, to stare at the paparazzi-snapped picture of a bikini-clad Eriadne Bellefort in Jay's arms in the deep blue waters of the Italian Riviera.

The phone rang. Robin. Grayson sighed as he answered.

"You knew, didn't you? How could you let him do this?" she rattled. "Jay told me you gave him directives to head to London to consult with some brokers there. But it was just a ruse, to dupe me. He's been with that slut all this time in Italy."

"Robin, calm down. You're gonna give yourself a heart attack if you don't chill out a little."

"I don't care! I thought things were over between them. How could you encourage him to go seek her out again?"

"I didn't encourage him—"

She snorted, loudly.

"—but you know as well as I do he's got to want to leave her."

Robin sighed. "And until then, she'll keep playing him like the lovesick idiot he really is."

Taking a deep breath, Grayson forced himself to blank his mind as he tried to calm Robin down and cover up for Jay. All in a day's work, and much of his daily job, actually. Back here, he didn't miss the high drama of the Manhattan office, but he couldn't say he didn't yearn for a little bit of the madness, too. For the past fourteen years, Jay and Robin had been his family, and he could never cut ties with them.

So where did it leave him? On one hand, he wanted to do more for the ranch, and on the other, he didn't want to leave the other life he'd known behind.

What embodied the middle ground, the compromise?

After ending the call, Grayson pocketed the phone, and glanced up at the field where joyous cheers resounded. Shayne had just scored a goal, it seemed. Her teammates ran up to her for a celebratory hug, and she radiated joy and carefree abandon in the way she jumped up and down, a wide smile on her face.

One thing he knew for certain, he wanted her in his life.

He only needed to figure out what said life would be.

Shayne kept a close eye on Grayson. The distance between them grew into wider chasms, and she sighed. The British had elevated the banal act of chitchat to an art, and Shayne didn't know if she should be proud of being British or not. She'd make chitchat a whole form of expression in the past week with

Grayson. Who knew there could be so much to say or notice about the weather?

And the blasted bloke who kept frowning and glaring at her, but made no move to open up or talk.

Why should he, when she didn't give any opening? To talk about their kiss would mean to talk about the future. Something even Grayson wouldn't want to acknowledge. Her future lay in Southall in another two months and a half. Full stop. Grayson's brought him back in New York.

From where she stood on the makeshift football pitch, she could see him leaning onto the corral's fence. His face grew dark, shuttered, and when he glanced in her direction again after cutting a call and pocketing his phone, his frown deepened. Blast, why did the man frown so much? He'd soon need Botox to erase all those worry lines on his face.

She fell into step with the girls as they walked toward the main ranch house. Grayson took off in the direction of the stables. Good, she wouldn't have to talk to him.

How much of an idiot was she, really? To get embroiled with a man without both of them agreeing to the terms of a transient, no-strings-attached affair? She'd already crossed the line into dangerous territory. By not setting up the boundaries right away, she'd tumbled headfirst into the churning waters of emotional attachment. Bloody hell, she fell in love with him.

Why don't you leave, Grayson, once and for all, so I can nurse my battered heart without the sight of you popping up everywhere around me?

She sounded like a Bollywood drama queen. Surely, she'd be made of sterner stuff than this? A man turned her to mush and she chose to stay mush? No way. *Get a grip on yourself, girl.*

With a resolute sigh, she broke away from the gaggle of high-pitched, squealing tweens.

"Same time tomorrow, Shayne?" Marion asked.

She nodded. Coming to a stop on the back porch, she blinked at the sight of the girls. How on earth did she get roped into coaching them? She recalled Marion knocking on the ranch's kitchen door on the afternoon of that fateful kiss. The tomboy asked if Shayne would mind tossing a ball around with her outside. To get her thoughts off Grayson and the scorching moment earlier, she'd agreed.

But how had one occurrence of tossing a football around turned into her coaching at least nine little girls? Seemed to her that every day, Marion brought more friends with her. Too eager to obliterate the thought of Grayson, and the possibility of bumping into him on the ranch, she'd plunged into the game. Running around and having her focus on the ball allowed her to spend the pent-up energy in her. Working inside the kitchens all day did nothing to make her destress, so sport it had to be to let her unwind.

Except that she had wound herself into another tight spot. She wouldn't be here for much longer, so who'd coach these girls once she left? A lot of them showed tremendous potential, which could only come out when nurtured by a coach who knew what she was doing.

Shayne bit back a groan when she stepped into the kitchen. Flame-haired Lynn Gilmore sat at the table with Aurelie. Over the past week, she'd become friends with Lynn. She'd also figured out the woman, though a total darling, embodied bossy, set to get her way in everything. For her to be here today spelt trouble with a big T.

"Hey, honey," Lynn called out. "We were just talking about you."

"In positive light, I hope," Shayne mumbled as she grabbed a bottle of water from the fridge.

Lynn laughed. "Of course. I was telling Aurelie what a great job you've been doing with the girls."

Shayne nearly sputtered the gulp of water in her throat. She knew that tone—her mother used it all the time to butter her up before springing for the jugular.

"Whatever you have in mind, it's no," she said as she started out of the kitchen.

"Damn it. How did you know I would ask you something?"

Lynn caught up with her on the threshold of the kitchen. "You wouldn't happen to have an easy-peasy recipe for chicken, would you? We're going through a phase with Elise and chicken is the only thing she'll eat. I'm sick and tired of the stuff I already know how to cook."

Why did she have the feeling this is not what the woman had planned to ask? There existed a glint in her green eyes, as well as the dejection of a harried mum on her tired features.

How could she deny her plea for help?

Simple. She couldn't. Shayne sighed again. "Will Elise eat anything with spices?"

She'd met the five-year-old, who'd struck her a terribly fussy eater, the kind with the potential to become a spectacular food critic later.

"As long as it's chicken."

"Let me get a shower. I'll be down in a few."

Aurelie jumped to her feet and all but happy-hopped to the doorway. "Can I record it?"

"To upload it within the upcoming hour on the vlog?" Her weariness resonated through every word in the question. "Isn't the channel for Indian sweets?"

"No, silly. It's for the food *you* prepare as the chef. Let me go get the camera." Reminding Shayne of a bouncy rabbit, Aurelie disappeared down the stairs to the basement.

Shayne went up, showered, and came back down dressed in comfy jeans and a short-sleeved T-shirt. Thanks to her daily morning outings, she no longer felt the drying effects of the Wyoming air. Her skin still needed more moisturizer than back home, and her hair, when not coiled into a tight bun, developed static energy. Lynn had pointed her toward a very good leave-in conditioner, which left her tresses manageable on most days.

Thanks to Grayson, she no longer cursed the Freewill atmosphere. He'd thought about her, tried to ease her plight, by taking her out on the second morning after his arrival.

He'd done so much for her—*Don't go there!* She couldn't afford to, not if she didn't want to turn into a mushy, goopy mess.

She forced her mind to go blank as she left the stairs and stalked to the kitchen. Lynn sat at the table.

"Can I lend you a hand?" the redhead asked as she stood.

"Just watch. This is a really easy dish."

"What's it called?"

"Easy-peasy chicken?"

"Are you telling me this is one of your own creations?"

"Yup."

"I just cannot wait. What do we need for it?"

She recited the list of ingredients as she grabbed them one by one and got on with her *mise en place*. "Chicken, onions, cardamom, *garam massala*, paprika, salt, tomato puree, and cream."

"That's it? And what's *garam massala*?"

She chuckled. "*Massala* means blend of spices in Indian language. *Garam* means hot. But *garam massala* is not about ulcer-provoking hotness. It's more a sort of warm, wholesome body given to a dish." She grabbed the tight-lidded jar with the spice and brought it to Lynn's nose. "Take a whiff."

"Hmm. It smells divine. What's in it?"

"Most cooks have their own blend. I use cardamom, cinnamon, coriander seeds, cumin, star anise, cloves, and little black pepper in mine. Just dry roast everything in a pan on low heat for about fifteen to twenty minutes, until it gets fragrant. Next, you grind it into a powder. Most home cooks use an electric grinder. I find the aromas are more pungent and hearty when you use a good ol' mortar and pestle."

She proceeded to place all the ingredients on the table and turned to the rack above the counter to grab the knife, cutting board, skillet, and wooden spoon she'd need to complete the *mise en place*.

Next to her, Lynn had grown quiet. Usually bubbly and a chatty Cathy, this alerted Shayne to something being off with the other woman. "What's wrong?"

"Just...what you're doing for the girls."

Uh-oh. She's going to rope me into something.

"What about it?"

Lynn bit her lip. "I don't think you know how much you've helped Marion, how much you've helped us. I—" She paused, took a deep breath. "I didn't always walk on the right path. Not until Jed stepped into my life, actually. Thank goodness for him."

A sense of unease flittered down Shayne's back. "You don't have to tell me—"

"Stop. I want to." Lynn pulled in a long breath. "Marion had started to take a bad path. The same I'd been on. I had no idea how to get her off that track. Until you came in and started practicing with her. In the past week alone, she's changed back into the lovely little girl we all adore. I wanted to say thank you."

She hadn't done anything. Nothing as praiseworthy as Lynn made it sound. "You're welcome," she muttered.

"I know it's a lot to ask you—"

And here it comes. She stood straighter, stiffened her spine and shoulders.

"—but, for as much time as you'll be here, would you agree to coach the girls' soccer team?"

"I'm only here for the summer."

"We'll find someone in the meantime. There's this woman in Montana I've been talking with. She might be coming for the next school year. But please, Shayne. Don't let my Marion drift away again."

There thrummed so much heartfelt emotion in the request she couldn't *not* hear the plea, the desperation, the appeal of a mother asking for her child's salvation.

And she being such a sucker for emotional drama, Lynn had roped her in hook, line, and sinker. "Okay. I'll take on the team."

"I cannot believe you started without me again, bitch." Aurelie stormed into the kitchen like a Fury on crack.

And thank goodness for her intervention. She didn't want to dwell on what she'd taken onto her shoulders. Shayne had never asked to be mentor and guide to impressionable little girls. She was so not a good role model for any growing girl. Look at her today: thousands of miles from her home, in love with a man who would leave at any minute, wobbling the same as badly set jelly whenever she remembered the blazing touch of his lips on hers.

No, definitely not adult behavior to emulate.

അ

For the rest of the afternoon, she lost herself in preparing the dish. As usual, she ended up making food for an army. Tracy Parks had, what seemed at the time, the perfect solution for their extra food—she invited the Gilmores over. Yet, dinner almost turned into a catastrophe as Shayne found out Lynn wasn't kidding when she complained her husband ate more than a herd of horses. Though tall, buff, and broad, where did Jedediah Gilmore pack all that food?

Lynn made them laugh when the Gilmores were leaving.

"Anytime you need a scavenger to scarf down your extra food, let me know, and I'll send Jed your way."

The object of the discussion turned a bright pink under his wife's teasing. For all he appeared to be a hulking giant, Jed Gilmore was in fact a sweet and gentle man who totally allowed himself to be bossed by his wife.

He seemed to adore Lynn, though, and his love appeared to be returned in kind. Shayne didn't miss the long, crackling-electricity look the married couple exchanged. A look excluding anyone but them in a silent, secret code only they knew.

Her heart clenched as she watched them. With their three daughters, the Gilmores appeared to her as the perfect family. Something she yearned to have…. A home, a man who would love her to the exclusion of anything else around them, the same man who would give her a brood of children and be by her side every step of the way to bring them up into wonderful adults.

She risked a glance at Grayson, at his departing back, in

fact. He and Jed were heading to the outback barn where the ranch hands lived. Something about poker night, Jed had said.

Could she have had everything she wanted with him?

Highly unlikely. He would head to New York soon; she'd be on her way to England in a few weeks. Both of them were in transit here in Freewill, on this ranch, in this world that could be a parallel universe to their respective daily existence.

Shayne bit her lip and turned from the porch. In her mind, she also turned her back to the receding-in-the-darkness form of Grayson Warner. Softly, she closed the door and started into the kitchen toward the stairs. She should check in for the night. The daily horse mounting turned her arse and hamstrings to battered, useless pieces of muscle, not helped by the relentless running on the pitch every afternoon. A wonder she hadn't torn a ligament yet.

She stood halfway through the corridor when the basement door slammed open with a crash. Shayne jumped two feet up in the air at the high-pitched squeal Aurelie let out as she tumbled out of the doorway and ran toward her.

"What in the bloody hell is wrong with you?"

"You are so not gonna believe this!"

"Believe what?" she asked once her heart had stopped racing. Adrenaline seemed to have pumped into her body when Aurelie had screamed and jumped onto her like a hyperactive zombie out for the kill.

Aurelie grabbed her shoulders. Shayne winced at the pain when the long fingers with the pointed nails dug into the flesh of her upper arms.

"Ever heard of World Global Network?" Aurelie asked.

"WGN, the Internet TV company?"

Aurelie nodded, her head bobbing so fast Shayne wondered whether the girl wouldn't snap her neck or something.

"I was just on the phone with them."

"Whatever for?"

Her friend grinned. "For the cooking show they are offering us on their network!"

Chapter Eight

"Keep your toes pointing up."

Shayne forced herself to breathe astride Bella while Grayson watched them from the other side of the corral's fence. She glanced down, checking if the reins sat in her grip as he'd showed her, her thumbs on top, with the strap flat between her pinkie and ring finger, and her hands low, close to the horse's shoulders.

Got this part.

"Shoulder, hip, and heel aligned," Grayson called out.

She sucked in her stomach, as she'd learned during those painstaking Pilates lessons her mother had dragged her to and that she'd abandoned after only two trips to the gym.

"Okay, stop the horse."

Still keeping her belly in, she sat her buttocks deeper into the saddle and tugged at the reins. Light grip, same force in both hands. Bella came to a stop, softly, and not in the abrupt way the first few times Shayne had tried to halt the animal. Seemed she was getting the hang of the whole riding business.

"Make her move again," Grayson hollered.

She pulled one rein and applied pressure with her calves.

"Break into a trot."

On a soft heel tap from Shayne, Bella started to trot,

stepping up the pace and throwing a lurching, side-to-side gait, under Shayne's haunches. They approached the fence, and she tried to make the horse shift direction. She yanked on the rein from the right side, to guide the animal's head right, in the direction to take. But the bloody thing kept moving forward. Even as she pulled harder, Bella refused to turn. "Why isn't she obeying?"

Her voice had grown panicky, which had the effect of making Bella break into a canter. The fence approached much faster.

"That's because you're not applying pressure with your outside leg."

Shayne released her hold on the rein, and pressed her left leg against the horse's side. Indeed, Bella heeded the subtle command and turned smoothly less than a yard from the fence.

"Whew. Close." She breathed out a sigh.

"You're doing great," Grayson cheered. "Now post the trot."

Oh blast. She'd start juggling this way and that on the horse. How did one post the trot? She focused to remember the instructions. *Rise in the stirrups at every other step. Keep the heel down, and keep contact with the horse's mouth.*

No bloody cowboy posted the facking trot, not in the Western way of riding a horse. But Grayson insisted they did things differently at Heart's Anchor. Everyone learned to ride the English way, with two hands on the reins and rising in the stirrups at every alternate clop during the trot. Easier to fall into the Western way of riding afterward. A bit like learning to drive a manual transmission and in the process, be able to handle an automatic gearbox. Not possible if one learned directly on an automatic transmission, same for the riding lessons. The ranch also boasted a few show-jumping champions, a technique that required riding the English way.

She lurched to the side and gripped the horse's mane to regain her balance. What did Grayson say? Horses trotted diagonally and not in a straight line? So she had to keep her eyes on the animal's shoulders, rise when the right shoulder was forward when moving right. Watch for the left shoulder going forward when moving left.

With a few deep breaths, she found the rhythm in the horse's gait. Soon, she posted her trot without much doubt she'd fall into an undignified heap on the dusty earth.

Maybe she would get the hang of it all.

Out of the corner of her eye, she watched Grayson go to the fence's gate and push it wide open.

Oh no. They were going outside the corral? She wasn't ready for this. She better calm down before she spooked the horse, though it took all her willpower to fight the overwhelming panic and appear composed.

"Wait," she called out.

A tall, beautiful, and lean black horse—the aptly named Black Beauty that she'd seen in the stables—pranced on the outer edge of the corral. When had a ranch hand brought him out? She hadn't noticed, focused on getting the lesson right.

Grayson checked the cinch on the Western saddle and, in one swift, graceful move, swung onto the animal's back. With a single shrug of his broad shoulders, he settled into place. The horse took a few steps, and man and beast flowed in synchronized movement on the spot.

She blanked out all cohesive thought at the sight, awed by the realization he did belong on a horse.

Until Bella mistook her relaxed stance for a cue and moved a step forward. Shayne tugged on both reins to stop the mare.

"Come join me," Grayson said.

Satisfied she had her mount under control, she risked a glance at him.

"Outside?" She shivered. "I'm not ready for this."

"Sure you are."

Laughter tinged his voice. What a change from the clipped tone of the previous days. What had happened to brighten his mood?

"Come on."

Compulsion laced those two words, a dare as well as an

invitation rolled into the soft tone. Something inside her fluttered, to gather nervous wings and break flight into her stomach. She couldn't deny she yearned to be with him, to do things with him, anything to allow them to spend time together. That's why she'd stuck to those bloody lessons, because they gave her a legitimate reason to be with Grayson every morning.

And where would he be taking her? Did he have something planned? She died to know.

The lethal curiosity won the better of her reticence, and she urged the horse forward until they stood outside the corral, next to Grayson and Black Beauty.

"You have to relax, Shayne. The poor animal is high-strung because of your nervousness."

Concentrated on accommodating the rolling gait of the creature, she didn't linger on the way her name sounded when it came out of his lips.

"I can't help it," she bit out.

"I told you, it's like sex. If you're tense, no one's gonna enjoy it."

She risked a glance at him all while heat flared through her and stung her cheeks. She remembered the first time he'd told her these words, the very first morning when he made Bella move around the corral, with her in the saddle. She'd tried hard to blank the images that burst into her mind at his comparison. Yes, sex needed relaxation and ease. Something chemistry with a partner brought to the equation.

What would Grayson bring if they ever had sex?

Heat, lasciviousness, abandon, intense pleasure. A lick of fire scorched through her when she encountered his narrowed gaze. She suddenly understood the allure of the cowboy with the wide-brimmed hat half shielding his face. The look was bloody sexy.

He urged his horse ahead. "Let's go."

She threw off the wicked daydreams in her head and set Bella forward. The thick mare fell into step behind the tall stallion. From where she sat, with her focus on Grayson's back, she couldn't tear her gaze off the easy way his hips rolled with the beast's movements. The two of them flowed similar to a unit, making one.

Exactly like sex made two bodies come together and flow as one. More heat seared her body. Try as she wished, she also couldn't stop pondering how sinful and graceful Grayson appeared on the stallion. The dark creature also looked beautiful, a fine example of horse masculinity. No female seeing them would ever be able to tear her eyes off the pair.

Shayne risked a glance at Bella, who trotted on ahead without once darting a glimpse at the stallion. Maybe the mare was menopaused, and she didn't recognize such a gorgeous specimen next to her.

Maybe she was simply sensible, too, knowing she could never dare compete out of her league with a horse that'd love her and leave her.

Do horses love and leave? She had to be going crazy.

Though she could do with some of her mare's brand of indifference. If Grayson no longer did anything to her pulse and her hormones....

He slowed his horse and turned around. The heated gaze he directed onto her made her gulp and tense up before she realized she should let her body flow loose and easy to not scare her mount.

"We should ride side by side. Not with you behind me."

She nodded as she caught up to him. He set his horse to match Bella's pace. Shayne kept the gait slow and controlled. It had to be hard for him to have to rein in his stallion so much. "Where are we going?"

"Just a little hike around the property. I wanted you to see it in the light of early morning."

Taking a deep breath to secure the knowledge she found her sync with Bella's trot, Shayne risked a glance at the surroundings. Wide, empty plains surrounded them, and a sort of dry, mulchy brown grass grew in patches over the land. In the distance, a range of softly rolling hills rose across the horizon.

The air crackled dry, with just a hint of the earth's wholesome scent on the clean oxygen it circulated all over the region. The overpowering horse scent melted in the outdoors, merging with the wind to bring a smell uniquely Wyoming to her nose. Silence, as if untouched by time, wrapped around them, broken now and then by the cheerful chirp of little birds.

Awed at the pristine, raw and wild beauty of the estate, she glanced over at Grayson. "It's beautiful."

"It does have this effect on most people."

She pointed toward the hills. "Is it where we're heading?"

"To the foot, yes. I'm not sure I want to let you loose on a trail hike just yet."

"I'm doing okay so far?" The question shot from her mouth before she could think it through. Blast, she had relaxed too much, it appeared.

"You're doing great."

There hung a soft, sizzling undertone to his words, and she made herself look ahead. Wouldn't do to misconstrue the path and fall off her horse, would it?

"Is all this land yours?" she asked.

"Pretty much, yeah. The Gaines family owns most of the ranch lands just on the edge of Freewill. My ancestors believed it'd be fair game to buy the land on the outer edge of the Gaines' territory, to not start a feud with them over the Freewill town boundary."

"Your ancestors have been here long, then."

"A bit less than two centuries. They came here in the eighteen forties."

"That's more time than my ancestors settling anywhere. The most I know about them takes us barely to the late eighteen hundreds."

"Where are you from, exactly?"

Bella's sturdy body rolled with a steady rhythm under her saddle. Shayne adapted to the gait and let the rocking movement carry her.

"Well, originally, my parents' grandparents were from India.

140

South Indians, Bengalis actually, from Calcutta. They left there toward the end of the nineteenth century, to immigrate to Mauritius."

"Where?"

She laughed, able to understand the incredulity in his tone. "Mauritius is a tiny island in the southern Indian Ocean, somewhere to the east of Madagascar. It used to be a French, then a British colony. In 1835, Britain abolished slavery on all its territories. The white landowners on the island however needed people to work the sugar cane fields, as sugar production was the main activity on the island."

"So they brought the Indians there?" Grayson asked.

"Exactly. From one British colony to the other. Indentured laborers, as they were known, or the less flattering term, coolies. They were told they weren't slaves, and they'd be paid to work the fields. They did get paid, a pittance. But what did they have waiting for them in India except poverty and death? So they worked the land on this unknown island, where they settled."

"Sounds like a toned-down version of the American dream."

The banter flowed easily between them, and she found him a rapt audience for her history cliff notes. Shayne loved to talk about Mauritius and her origins. Too bad she never had much of an opportunity to do so often.

They had reached the empty plains. The chirp of birds had faded, the reverent quiet in the air broken only by the clopping of their horses' hooves.

"It kinda was," she continued. "Mauritius is also a land of immigrants, and over time, those who had come to toil under the colonist regime rose to take the reins of power."

"They had a civil war?"

She laughed. "Nothing as drastic. Mauritius got its independence in nineteen sixty-eight, and became a republic in nineteen ninety-two. Political negotiations, all the way."

"So that's the story of your ancestors. What about yours?"

She risked a glance at him. He had his gaze on her, not needing to keep his eyes on the path. Reins firmly in the left hand, he steered and controlled his mount as if by instinct.

He was born here, and he belonged to this land. No matter how civilized Wyoming appeared today, a certain pulsating wildness, an edge of raw energy and the refusal to be tamed, echoed off the land.

Echoed off the people of this land. Off Grayson.

Her mouth went dry under his steady perusal. Here, he became a cowboy barely containing his soul's connection to the land. In his pulse beat the life of this earth, the riotous passion of this region.

Shayne forced her eyes away. He had her under his spell, and blast if that didn't make her wish with all her heart to give in to him.

The hills loomed closer. In the distance, they had appeared rolling and rather puny. But up close, some slopes seemed in fact quite steep, the others rambling climbs. The sun beat down hard on her shoulders, the warmth spearing to her skin and making her squirm.

"You're from England, aren't you?" Grayson asked.

She nodded. Good thing he'd brought the conversation back to the original topic. Here she sat forming silly ideas of love and attraction where he was concerned. Too much clean air, maybe. Her brain, used to pollution, scrambled from too much oxygen.

"Born and bred," she replied, and threw her shoulders back. Neutral ground, she reminded herself. "Guess they say the grass is always greener on the other side? The same thing that happened to my ancestors when they left India happened to a lot of Mauritians soon after the independence. Many struck it abroad, England, primarily, and Australia. My father moved first. Afterward, he went back to the island to get married to a girl he'd never met in an alliance my grandparents had arranged for him. Brought his bride back to England, settled in Southall, had two kids within the next decade." She shrugged. "And here I am."

A wisp of soft wind rushed around her. Shayne could swear she heard a woman's giggle. She frowned and tugged on the reins. Bella slowed her pace, and Grayson shot them a concerned glance.

"Sounds like a tale of fortitude," he said despite the narrowing of his eyes. "You ever been there?"

She was being silly. With a low, clucking sound, she made her horse pick up. "Been where?"

"Mauritius."

"A few times, to visit the family."

"And you liked it?"

"Why do you ask?"

"Because you come from all these different places. I know I come from the ranch; my family hasn't known anything but Heart's Anchor for the past one hundred and seventy years. While yours has hopped over three continents."

Shayne pondered his reasoning. She did come from all these places, but was she the sum of all the parts, or simply the product of her upbringing? "I'm British, Grayson. Born and raised in Southall, parts of me a Londoner. That's it."

She paused, glanced at the hills growing bigger, nearly into whole mountains, as they approached. "I liked Mauritius. Just like I liked India. I just never felt a kinship with these places. Home to me is Southall. Full stop."

"Home is where we wish it to be," he said softly.

The words carried on another soft wind to her. The breeze seemed to flitter around her shoulders, and it wrapped itself around her. Strands of her hair lifted from the locks broken free from her bun.

With an uncanny certainty, she recalled the morning in the kitchen when the ghost or spirit or whatever it had been, had danced around her. She was pretty sure the same entity flew around her in the form of the soft breeze. No wind seemed to play with the shaggy fringe on the front of Grayson's jacket.

No, must be her friendly ghost.

The laugh again. The same girlish giggle of before.

They had reached the foot of the hills. Where she'd apprehended their rising in front of her in a daunting wall of dry earth and rocks, she no longer felt any reluctance to head up their paths. Two trails beckoned, the one to the left appearing to be a shorter, straight path to the top of a hill.

What would it feel to climb up on horseback?

Listen to you. One ride and she already set out for adventure. Was she out of her mind? "Can we go up? What's over there?"

She steered Bella to the left and turned toward Grayson.

His face carried an odd combination of a dark frown in his eyes and on his forehead, with tension clamping his jaw and slashing his mouth to a thin line.

And then he trained his gaze on her. She thought she caught a flicker of sadness in their dark depths, but then the light chased it away.

"Caves," he said. "And I'd rather not go there, if you don't mind."

Something was wrong. "Okay."

Go to the right.

The low, girlish voice soothed through her mind. She heard the words as if someone whispered in her ear.

Was it the ghost?

The wind blew in her hair again, fluttering from the left, which made her turn her face right, toward the path, in Grayson's direction.

Her gaze traveled from one to the other all while her heart hammered and the rush and tug of blood at her temples shrouded her perception. Settling her focus on the trail, she saw it moved up, in a gentle, meandering path that dipped over the crest of a ridge above.

She pulled the rein on the right and pressed Bella's side with her outside leg. The horse turned right and started moving up the trail.

"Shayne? Where are you going?"

Grayson sounded worried, and she felt more than heard the big stallion fall into step behind her mare.

"You've never gone trail riding before," he urged.

But something inside her compelled her to move ahead. Certain of her seat, of her balance, and of her grip on the horse, all her riding inhibitions seemed to melt away. Nothing mattered but getting to the end of the trail.

"Do you know where it leads to?" she asked.

"Yes, but you're not ready yet—"

With a subtle press of her legs, she encouraged the horse to go faster. Within seconds, she cleared the ridge and started the descent on the other side of the hill. The path meandered left, flanking the hillside, and stood so narrow two horses couldn't ride abreast.

"Shayne, turn back now. Let's go down."

She kept her attention on the trail, though, compelled to do so by a certainty that made her heart race, knowing something awaited her beyond the bend.

"I want to see where it leads to," she called out, and steered the horse farther.

"Goddammit! Wait, I'm coming down, too."

She didn't pause, certain he would catch up easily. Which he did.

"You reckless damn woman! What compelled me to bring you out here today?"

"Oh, just shut up, will you? You're the one who said I'm no coward, and here I am proving it to you."

"Do you have to risk your neck to do that?"

They'd climbed up, still flanking the hillside. To their right, the ground dipped into a steep ravine. Only a hundred yards deep, someone could fall and break their neck down there.

Keep going, the voice whispered. *Just around the bend....*

The hill curved left some three hundred feet from them. Shayne couldn't see anything beyond the curve. Whatever awaited there?

"Careful around the bend," Grayson called out behind her.

She slowed Bella's pace, and negotiated the turn. The path hugged the hillside, but it followed a downward path that would take them around the hill and into another hidden curve.

When the trail flattened again, Shayne could swear she heard the murmur of running water. Pushing Bella forward, she bridged the last few feet to the bend and emerged on the other side of the craggy rock.

She drew in a shocked breath when her gaze alighted on the scenery before her. They'd ended at a secluded creek. A thin river gurgled, its bank a wide stretch of flat land covered in a carpet of green moss. The clear water lapped over rounded pebbles at the edge of the spit of land. Brilliant sunshine radiated all around, reflecting off the water it turned into a shimmery layer sparkling like crystal.

Home.

The word flittered in her mind, and the breeze blew in her hair again.

This is where the ghost had wanted to bring them. But why? Though the place looked gorgeous, what could be so special about it? How did she explain the atmosphere of hushed reverence hovering over the whole spot and reminding her of a shroud of peace?

Maybe if she stepped on the ground, she would know.

Shayne removed her feet from the stirrups. Grasping the saddle, she did the whole mounting procedure in reverse, and jumped off the animal.

Her booted feet landed with a muffled thud on the thick moss. Spying a sturdy tree nearby, she grasped Bella's reins and tied them to a branch. The first thing Mika had told her when he watched her descend from the horse one day—how she should always secure the reins so the animal wouldn't ride off.

Grayson dismounted, too, and tied Black Beauty to the tree. But her attention wasn't on him. She could see nothing except the clear water rolling on the riverbed. Would it taste as sweet and refreshing as it seemed?

"Damn it, Shayne! You scared the life out of me back there," Grayson shouted behind her.

She gave him a cursory glance, enough to notice the fury on his face, unmarred by the hat he'd let fall to the ground.

"The creek is beautiful," she heard herself saying.

"Are you out of your mind?" He grabbed her arm in a crushing hold and turned her to face him. "If you'd fallen off that ledge—"

"I didn't fall."

"Damn you." His eyes narrowed, nostrils flared, and he clamped his hand on her arm stronger.

This should hurt, she remembered thinking, but all thoughts shattered when he tugged her to him hard and crushed her mouth with his.

The banked fire she hadn't been able to put out soared into a blazing inferno the minute she opened her lips and returned his kiss. With his arms around her waist, he pulled her flush against his body as he plundered her mouth with his tongue. Shayne met him thrust for thrust, her own passion overflowing and telling her she'd die if she didn't have this man right there on the spot.

She trailed her hands under the lapels of his jacket and pushed the heavy garment off his shoulders. The warmth of his skin seared her palms through the thin cotton of his T-shirt, and she couldn't wait to get the clothes off him, to feel his naked skin and experience the scorch of his touch.

Grayson groaned when she ran her fingers under his T-shirt to caress his chiseled torso. He worked in an office, for goodness' sake. How could he have such rock-hard abs? His chest felt smooth under her touch, not even a smattering of hair. She craved to run her tongue over his pecs, to dip them in the ridges of his six-pack, to suck his tightened nipples into her mouth before she'd softly bite them with her teeth.

Heat wrapped her, and warm moisture gushed from her core at the lascivious images that painted themselves in her mind. Shayne tugged his T-shirt off, at the same time she pressed her lower body to his thighs and let the hard bulge in his jeans nestle against her belly.

They had to stop the kiss while he ditched the garment. Grayson settled a hand on her jaw, and he brought her back toward him so he could kiss her again. His openmouthed kisses made a feminine instinct inside her know he couldn't get enough of her; at the realization, she smiled against his mouth.

Oh, how she wanted him. Desire didn't start to describe the craving she felt for Grayson. More like a soul-deep yearning, a blistering need to be whole and complete, at last.... And since he'd kissed her again, taken the first step, no way in hell would she let him go.

She pulled her lightweight jumper over her head. Snaking her hand in Grayson's hair, along the nape of his neck, she brought his head down until he could nuzzle her throat. With his tongue, he explored the dip in her collarbone. A soft sigh escaped her, because she wanted more, despite the sensation she could die already from his touch and go to heaven right away. She released her grip on his slightly shaggy hair, to trail both hands down his solid, muscled back.

How could an office potato pack so much hard, warm muscle on his gorgeous frame?

The question evaporated when he kissed the valley between her breasts, pushed up by her La Senza bra. He licked her skin there, freeing the soft flesh from the lacy cups that he replaced with his opened hands.

When he closed his moist lips on her nipple, Shayne gasped. Her knees went weak, and she clung to his shoulders to stay upright. *God Almighty.* If he could do so much to her just by worshipping her breasts, how would it feel to have him thrusting inside her?

She had to know. With nimble fingers, she reached down to the buttons on her jeans and shucked the garment down with her knickers, tearing the big boots off in the process. After undoing the clasp of her bra, she ditched the lace scrap and attacked Grayson's waistband. While she tugged with the button and zipper, he reached into his back pocket and pulled a small foil rectangle. Good, he came prepared.

Did he know they'd make love today? No, he couldn't, because the ghost had prompted her to come here, not Grayson.

Who cares? Nothing mattered except that he seemed as eager for her as she was for him, and blast if she'd let him get away.

Naked against her, skin to skin, he molded her body to his before he captured her mouth again. Shayne surrendered. The taste of him filled her like an aphrodisiac, as much a drug to make her forget everything as a remedy to make her feel alive, every single cell of her.

One arm on her waist, the other hand clasping a buttock, he leaned forward into her. She wasn't afraid she'd fall; she understood he wanted her to go down. She went, and indeed, he didn't let her fall. The bed of moss felt cool against her skin, not the startling shock of cold she'd expected to experience. The warm sun rays danced on the front of her body. Grayson rolled over her and replaced the heat with his own. Shayne arched into his body.

He trailed his mouth down her neck, onto her breasts. Then he danced his tongue in long, slow licks along her stomach. Her body rose up to get closer to his, and she stifled giggle; she was doing a perfect plank. *So that's where they come handy.*

Fire burned in sizzling sparks from low in her belly, the same spot where he licked and nipped the soft flesh with his mouth.

Bloody hell, she'd forgotten about the spare tire around her lower belly, the one merging with her love handles. He'd run away once he realized what he kissed. And no way would she let him escape without taking her, at least once. If she didn't make love to Grayson Warner, she'd regret it her whole life.

With suppleness and strength she pulled from God knew where, she tucked a leg around his thigh and pushed him over until she straddled him. Her hair hung in loose locks around her face, the elastic holding them back somewhere in the bun that had broken into a ponytail.

Grayson snaked a hand along her nape, and with deft fingers, released her hair until the long, straight strands danced over her shoulders and down her back. Without letting go, he pulled her down, to meet her halfway for a searing kiss that sent shards of pleasure all the way to her toes. She kissed him in return, before she remembered her purpose. Breaking free, she pushed him flat on his back and darted her tongue out to taste the skin in the dip of his throat.

The low rumble of his groan, right against her open mouth, coursed with the potency of an accelerant blazing her inner fire to new heights. His skin tasted salty, and smelled of soap and male sweat.

Best scent ever. His pecs were smooth, his nipples pebbled tips against her moist lips. The evidence of his desire pulsed hot and hard against her belly, and she couldn't wait to have him inside her. At the imagined pleasure that nearly sent her orgasm skyrocketing without him even touching her, she closed her teeth on his nipple.

He gave a sharp intake of breath, his body rising to press against hers.

Grayson proved swift and supple—in one move, he had her onto her back and pinned his knee between her parted thighs. He reached for the condom and sheathed himself.

Shayne opened her thighs wider when he settled between them. She sighed in bliss. Nothing like the feel of a man's body over one's own. His weight, which could easily crush her but that instead softly pressed her down. His strong arms enclosing her between them when he leaned on his forearms. The smell of his sweat and their combined arousals wafting to her nose. Knowing how, with a simple lift of her head, she could claim his mouth and welcome his tongue. Exactly the same way she'd hug his sides with her thighs as she urged her core against his engorged cock.

He pushed one hand between them, until his fingers touched her moist sex. Grayson didn't pull back, though. He stroked and teased, made her even more ready for him.

She reveled in all these sensations and sighed against his mouth when he slid inside her. Hot, hard, throbbing. The condom did nothing to numb the feel of him as he completed her and merged his body to hers.

Then he fitted in to the hilt, and he rocked his hips against hers. She responded in kind, letting her body get accustomed to the rhythm with which he took her, retreated, to take her again. Pleasure built crescendo inside her, from deep between her legs, coursing up until every muscle grew high-strung, awaiting deliverance that would wash over her when her orgasm crashed. Shayne arched her back, her abdomen coming into contact with his. Grayson dipped his head to her chest, and caught a nipple between his lips.

When he closed his teeth on the tightened bud, as she'd done to him, she abandoned herself, let go completely. Her orgasm shattered through her as if every cell had burst with an energy it could no longer contain.

Free-falling despite his arms bracketing her, despite the mossy carpet under her back, her eyes flew open to stare at his bent head. As if he felt her stare, he peered up, and she found herself committing the memory of his passionate gaze and the coiled tension on his features into her heart.

Never had a man looked at her with such intensity when he took her, neither had she abandoned herself to someone as she'd done with him.

Communion. That's what they'd had.

As the certainty settled around her mind like a flutter of delicate muslin, the way her heartbeat had soared to calm down could mean only one thing. She was meant to be with Grayson.

And, though realizing this for the first time in her life, panic didn't grab her. Instead, a strange, soothing peace descended.

Grayson stilled. "What is it?"

"I love you."

Had he heard her right? He sought her gaze, searching for the confirmation of the words he'd probably imagined she'd said.

Then he saw it, in the way she parted her lips, how her breath quickened, how her eyes widened, as if she herself hadn't realized what she'd disclosed.

Before she could panic, retract the confession, brush the words off, and crumble him to a pile of dry dust, he kissed her.

Would it be melodramatic of him to believe something vital flowed into him through one single touch of their mouths? Because that's exactly what he felt, like a gentle wisp of life traveled through every inch of him when he kissed her. Offered him rebirth. Made him feel whole again.

His body prompted he still lay buried inside her, on the brink of release. He'd fathomed he loved her even prior to getting off. What did it say about the strength of his feelings for her?

But he hovered on the brink, and the need to lose himself inside her overcame him. One move of his hips, and intense pleasure racked through his whole being.

He'd made love to other women in the past, women who'd told him they loved him after they had climaxed.

But with Shayne, everything was different. Unique. A moment where time had stopped and where history—*their* history—wrote itself.

He tore his mouth from hers. She hitched in a breath, her lips parted, still moist from their passionate kiss. Her eyes clouded over. Doubt? Regret?

Never. She'd been the best experience of his entire existence, the one spot of brightness in thirty-two years of an abyss that just got darker and darker.

Propping himself on a forearm, he reached up with his other hand to brush her hair from her temple. Then, he stared into her eyes.

"I love you, too."

He'd never said those words, always believing he wouldn't be able to feel them for someone else, let alone pronounce them out loud.

To say this phrase to her changed everything, at the same time his whole world settled on its axis. This represented where he was meant to be. Home, on the ranch, with Shayne.

She smiled, and he wanted to let out a very macho, and

totally unlike him, whoop of successful conquest when the happiness radiated over her face and lit her golden skin as if from within. She'd never appeared more beautiful, and her beauty, everything in her, and the way she gave herself to him humbled him. Grayson pressed a kiss to her forehead. Wrapping his arms around her, he rolled them until they lay on their sides. He slipped out of her in the movement, and after ditching the soiled condom to the side, pulled her to him again.

Shayne tucked her head in the crook of his shoulder. Her thick hair tickled his neck, and he reached up to brush the locks back and cradle her jaw against his palm.

She placed her hand on his and threaded their fingers together. Warm sunlight bathed over them, the sound of gurgling water ensconcing them in a bubble where time, and reality, had no grip.

He wanted to stay this way forever and never let Shayne go.

But the thought slithered into his mind nevertheless. She would leave in a few weeks, and his life waited for him back in New York.

Not if he could help it.

Maybe the time had come for him to make peace with his demons, the ones waiting for him on the other side of the hill, on the trail he'd told Shayne led to the caves. His parents' graves. Until he went there, he wouldn't be able to strive for a clean start. He also had to talk to Jay and Robin, find a way to work out how he could come back here and not put the firm in jeopardy. He owed his friends the truth, about why he became how he was today.

He and Shayne couldn't have a future until he'd come clean from his past.

A matter of a couple of weeks. A quick trip to New York and coming back here. Until then, he wouldn't promise Shayne anything. She deserved the truth, too, but he owed it more to his best friends who'd been through thick and thin with him for the past fourteen years.

How to get Shayne to stay put, and wait for him, without

letting her in on his secrets right away?

Then he remembered. There existed a way.

He pressed a kiss to her hair. "Aurie said you're not going to do the cooking show."

She stiffened in his arms, and broke free from his embrace. Then she glanced at him, frowning, shook her head, and laughed.

"What's so funny?" he asked as he propped himself on an elbow.

"Nothing. You just really know how to kill the teenage dream mood."

"Teenage dream?"

"You haven't listened to the Katy Perry song? As how this girl is saying that when her man loves her the way he does, she feels like she's living a teenage dream, the embodiment of all she'd fantasized love would be when she was a teen?"

He frowned. Shayne, a teenybopper? What else was she into? Miley Cyrus? "I'm afraid my music tastes are a bit on the opposite end of the spectrum."

She flopped onto her belly, next to him, giving him a world-class view of her lush hips and the bootylicious curve of her ass. "Damn, babe. You've got one hell of an ass."

The sound of her full-bodied laughter zinged through him like the jolt of much-needed caffeine after a sleepless night. He smiled, and his smile grew wider when she blushed under the reverent touch of his hand on one cheek of her perfect buttocks.

He'd almost forgotten what they were talking about. Grayson placed his hand in the small of her back. "Why did you say no to the show?"

The laughter died on her features, and she shrugged. "I just don't feel it's really me."

"Why not?" He danced the tips of his fingers against her skin, teasing the two deep dimples at the top of her backside.

"Because I'm not good at it. That's why."

He stilled. Shayne thought she wasn't good at what she did? Where did the woman pull such crap into her mind? He trailed his hand up her back, until he cradled the nape of her neck in his palm.

"Listen to me. I've seen those videos. You are goddamned fabulous at what you do."

She blushed, and lowered her gaze. "I'm not."

She wasn't playing coy; too much skepticism in those two words. "Believe me. I never knew how to hone a knife before you showed it during one video."

"The trick of angling the blade at twenty degrees against the stone? It's basic knowledge."

"At culinary school, maybe. Not for the rest of us." He paused. "You're a great chef, Shayne."

"I never wanted to be a chef, you know."

"So why did you do it?"

"Let's just say I've got very old-fashioned parents who think a girl's place is in the household or the kitchen, and the only necessary skills she needs are cooking and knowing how to mend a sock." She tilted her head down, which made her hair fall in a curtain concealing her features when she next spoke. "Choosing to go to culinary school was the lesser of the battles, so I went in order to get them off my back."

Push came to shove. But it didn't mean she sucked at what she did.

"Look at me," he said as he reached for her chin and made her lift her head in his direction. "You might've felt cornered, but one doesn't get to where you are today without determination and talent. You have what it takes to be everything you set your heart on."

She gave a soft laugh. "A TV celebrity chef? Is this really what I want?"

"How can you know if you don't try it?"

Grayson wanted to believe her silence meant she pondered his words. He cupped her cheek and brushed her lips with his thumb.

He wanted this woman to have the world at her feet, wanted the world to see how fabulous she was.

155

And he also wanted to keep her busy and in Freewill for the coming two weeks.

Two weeks. Not much to ask, right?

He gazed into her eyes, saw the glinting depths of emotion rolling inside her right then, as well as the doubt.

Grayson bent his head, to drop a light kiss on her lips. "I trust you."

She ran the tip of her tongue against her lower lip, made to look even fuller thanks to his ardent kisses. Another macho whoop of triumphant conquest almost escaped him.

"Okay," she said. "I'll do it."

Victory. He smiled, and kissed her, deeper this time.

Everything would work out, once he took one thing at a time.

Chapter Nine

Grayson couldn't say what hit him first when he stepped out of the cab a few blocks from his apartment building in New York a few days later. The smells or the sounds? The clogging scent of exhaust fumes, and near the mouth of a subway station, the unique, distinctive smell of metal and oil of the subway cars. The ammonia-tinged reek of urine from dark corners bothered him less, since he'd grown used to the earthy smells of horse and manure and earth back in Freewill.

The drone of traffic and blaring horns hurt his brain after the quiet of the Wyoming plains broken only by the chirp of little birds. All around him, voices rose in a cacophony of accents and languages while high heels clopped the pavement with a solid tread. Amidst the crowds, whiffs of expensive perfume touched his nostrils, merging with the warm aroma of fresh bagels and coffee when he passed beside the neighborhood Starbucks and the little café a few doors from it.

One scent really slammed home—the warm, sugary odor wafting from the nuts vendor on the curb. The sweet whiff washed over him and his step lurched when the memory of Shayne, and how she always smelled of slightly burned sugar, crashed and made him yearn for her with a force that squeezed inside his chest.

He'd had three perfect days, and nights, with her. They'd

kept their affair on the down low; he didn't want anyone to look at her oddly for being his lover or tease her before he could be there to make their relationship official, to state to Freewill at large that she was his as he belonged to her. His aunt sent him quizzical glances, and he'd caught her indulgent smile when he'd stared at Shayne a little too long at the breakfast table. Thank goodness Aurelie still stayed in the dark; otherwise the news of them hooking up would've been plastered over the Net within the blink of an eye.

One thing at a time, he reminded himself as he stood at the floor-to-ceiling window in his apartment, staring at the view of Central Park while twilight darkened the air.

His hand itched to reach for the phone and call Shayne. It would be late afternoon in Freewill, though, a time when she would most probably be in the kitchen at Heart's Anchor, which WGN had turned into its studio to shoot the show featuring Shayne and Aurelie. He'd met the production team and seen how they steamrolled their way in. Shayne would have her hands full with them, and he wouldn't add to her burden by disturbing her on the set.

He also had something more important to do. He'd come straight here after his plane landed and had called Jay, who'd reached New York under the glare of paparazzi flashes with Eriadne two days earlier, and Robin to tell them he'd returned and needed to talk to them. They'd agreed to come over in the evening, and he waited for them.

As if on cue, the elevator dinged and the doors slid open to let his business partners into the penthouse.

Grayson frowned when his gaze alighted on them. The wide chasm between the two jumped evident to the naked eye. Robin had lowered her head and sent Jay venom-filled glances from under her lashes. Damn, she drove Grayson crazy with her habit of peering up through the long, blonde bangs that reached well below her eyebrows. He didn't know a woman who could chastise a man so well simply with a glance.

She flew to him. "Gray!"

Her voice sounded unusually throaty, and he took a whiff at her hair when she embraced him. He only smelled shampoo, but it could mean she'd concealed the evidence of cigarettes in her life.

"You've started smoking again, haven't you?" he asked when she released him.

"'Course not."

"Then why is your voice pitch back to how it was when you grilled four packs a day? You know the doctor told you to ditch the sticks, or you'd be signing your own warrant for a heart attack." He turned to Jay. "You didn't notice she started smoking again? Man, I left her in your care."

"Well, he hasn't been around, has he? Does he effing care? Fucking no!"

Jay thrust his chin forward. His body, with the tense shoulders and rigid spine, stood braced for a fight.

Grayson shook his head. He didn't need this. "What is it with you two?"

Robin glared as she brushed past him to reach the couch, where she flopped down. "Don't ask me. Ask *him.*"

"How the hell will I know, when she won't even talk to me since I got back?"

"Guys." Grayson sighed.

Jay thumped him on the shoulder. "Good to have you back, man." He paused. "You don't look any worse for the wear, so I gather the trip home went well?"

"It would help your conscience, wouldn't it? After you all but fed me to the wolves there."

"He doesn't have a conscience," Robin stated.

Jay snarled at her as he sat on the couch opposite hers.

"Don't you think you're coming down a bit hard on him?" Grayson asked.

"Yeah, Robin. Cut it out already, will you?" Jay added.

"Oh, shut up. I'm not talking to you."

"Really?" Jay scooted to the edge of the seat. "Guess what? You just did, Bibi."

Robin jumped to her feet. "Don't you dare call me that stupid name."

"Bibi, you just spoke to me again." Jay grinned.

Robin clenched her fists; she'd fly at Jay within the next few seconds. How had he forgotten these two could bicker more than Shayne and Aurelie? He reached for Robin and pulled her back with one arm across her chest. "Stop it, both of you. We need to talk."

His serious tone must've done the trick, because both dropped their glares to stare at him. Robin sat down with a *plop* and frowned when she pinpointed her sparkling blue eyes on him. Jay's jaw looked clamped, his dark eyes narrow.

"What are you going to spring on us?" Jay asked. "I thought your return to Freewill went well."

"It did." *Too well, in fact.* He went back to the window and stared out. "I never told you the reason I left Freewill and why I never went back."

"It has to do with your parents' deaths, right?" Robin spoke first.

"There's a bit more than that."

"What do you mean?" Jay asked.

He forced himself to take a deep breath. The time had come for full disclosure.

"The Warners have been in Freewill since before the Civil War. The land has passed from father to son for five generations," he started. "My father was the third son, with no hope he'd ever inherit, and it suited him perfectly. He always had his head in the clouds, and at a hippie community in New Jersey, he met my mother and married her. Shortly after, both his brothers died, and he found himself the last Freewill Warner. The ranch became his, and they moved to Wyoming, where I was born."

"What happened after? You once said...." Robin trailed off.

Jay cleared his throat. "That your father killed your mother," he finished for her.

Grayson winced at the lance of pain shooting through his

jaw. He had to do this, to put the demons to rest. Talking about it would be the first step.

"Bobby Warner never grew up. That's why the hippie lifestyle suited him so well. So easy to get high and not bother with anything else. He reeled my mother into his philosophy, too. I grew up more in the households of the ranch hands and their families than in my own. My father wouldn't stand for anything, or anyone, taking her attention away from him. To ensure her compliance, he kept her high all the time. I grew up thinking the smell of pot was normal in a house, the way the other houses smelled of pine-scented cleaner or lemon polish."

He paused for a few seconds. "He resented me for taking her away from him, even a little. The more I grew up, the more he'd pull her into his warped world. One day when lucid, my mother complained of pain in her chest, along her breast. I urged her to go see a doctor, but he heard us and flew into a rage. To stop him from hitting me, my mother threw herself at his feet and pledged to be with him every single minute if he left me alone."

"Gray," Robin murmured as she stood.

"It's not over yet, hon. Let me tell you the rest." He took a deep breath. "It turns out the pain represented an early symptom of breast cancer. To keep my father away from me, my mother gave in to his addiction. She was always high, so damn high she never realized how much her health had deteriorated. Nothing existed beside the two of them."

His throat closed, and he swallowed, hard, beyond the lump. Robin placed her hand on his shoulder from behind.

"I called my aunt one day, and she came over from California. Took over everything. But for my mother, we were too late. The cancer had metastasized, spread through her whole body, even reaching her bones. The same perdition she was led into became her salvation, because when she was high, she didn't feel the pain, didn't feel the cancer consume her slowly."

A tear slipped down his cheek when he recalled her brief bouts of lucidity, when she'd cry out for him, begged him to not leave her. At first, being at the ranch, he saw her in every corner of the big house, heard her hoarse cries. But the more he drew close to Shayne, the less he saw her face wherever he turned, until she became simply a memory that stabbed his heart but nevertheless released him from its grip.

All thanks to Shayne. He missed her and wanted to tell her all this, open up to her.

Robin hugged him from behind, settled her cheek between his shoulder blades. To have her comfort, like that of a sister, soothed him. He couldn't do this alone.

"She died in her sleep, I hope peacefully. And when she was gone, my father seemed to wake up from his stupor. His first words were to curse me for having taken her away from him, before he crumbled to his knees and begged me to tell him how he could continue living without her."

He shook with the memory. Tremors coursed through him, and his chest hurt. He didn't need to close his eyes to recall this big, strong man on the floor, glaring up at him with so much desperation in his eyes. Eyes he saw whenever he glimpsed into a mirror, at the reflection of the same face and body, since he'd grown up into the spitting image of Bobby Warner.

"What did you do?" Jay asked.

He turned around, pulling Robin under his arm to clutch her close. "Nothing. He killed himself on the eve of her funeral, left a note as to how he wished to be with her, even in death."

Jay had paled. "Gray, I didn't know, man. If I did, I'd never have forced you to go back."

Robin released him to stare at Jay. "What do you mean, force him to go back?" She turned back to Grayson. "You didn't go to Freewill willingly?"

"Jay kinda twisted my arm, but he did a good thing. High time I faced my past. I thought I was like my father, but I found out I'm not. I'm nothing like him."

"Of course you aren't. We already knew that. You poor darling," she cooed, before she wrapped her arms around his neck and hugged him tight. She eased her hold on him to glance at Jay. "Oh, come here, you big dumb lug."

Grayson's gaze met Jay's, and he rolled his eyes. Robin and her group hugs. But Jay came forward anyway and let her wrap one arm around his neck as she pulled them both in her embrace.

Peace, reminding him of the kind he'd felt with Shayne in the creek, settled over him and calmed the riot of emotions that had brewed up in his body, in his memories. He'd owed his best friends—the siblings he'd never had—the truth, and to give it to them proved nothing short of liberating for him. He squeezed the two of them, and dropped a kiss on Robin's hair.

They ended the embrace, each taking a step back.

"So, what happens now?" Jay asked.

No more beating around the bush.

"I'm moving back to Freewill. We need to discuss how to keep the firm going, or if we'll have to disband."

೧೮

"I want something new, something fresh, something never done before. I need to wow the audience, to give them *unique.*"

And what else do you want with that? My firstborn?

Shayne glared at Katya, the production manager WGN had assigned her. Barely three weeks around the woman and she found herself ready to commit murder. Nothing was ever good enough, or unique enough, for the bloody producer.

Katya paced the Heart's Anchor kitchen while Shayne sat at the table, watching her wear down paths in the linoleum tiles with her endless walking. Katya could never sit or stand still, it seemed. Her mouth, too, always moved, either chastising Shayne or some poor soul at the other end of her BlackBerry.

Katya stopped, which alerted Shayne to something bad happening very soon. The woman's razor-cut blonde bob moved with the abrupt halting, while the thick, black frame of her glasses stayed put on the bridge of her obviously remodeled nose. Katya hailed from Los Angeles, the land where plastic surgery accompanied skinny nonfat lattes like the McDonald's counter girl asking if "you'd like a side of fries with your order?"

"That thing you did with the pink icing." Katya pinpointed her piercing dark eyes on Shayne. "What ever was it?"

A measure of gratitude and relief slid through her when Aurelie joined her at the table. Katya didn't seem to notice the other girl had sat down. Similar to an eagle, when her focus directed onto something, or someone, nothing else existed.

Too bad Shayne became the recipient of the attention. If she'd known agreeing to do the show, the twelve episodes the network had ordered, would land her in Katya's forced proximity, she would've said no.

Instead, she had listened to Grayson, believed him when he bolstered her self-esteem by telling her she was a good cook who should grab the show with open hands.

How will you know if you don't try?

Those words echoed in her head all the time. And she'd tried the cooking show. Some days she loved; others she loathed the endeavor. They'd shot every single afternoon for the past three weeks. Katya had more than twelve episodes she could put together. But was the woman satisfied? Bloody no. She wanted Shayne to be more "unique."

Stuff "unique." She'd had it up to here with being original. She didn't think she'd ever say these words but give her back her restaurant kitchen with its fixed menu Aunt Shilpa had refused to alter even when fresh produce for the dishes came in short supply.

"Are you listening to me?" Katya snapped her fingers in front of Shayne's face, tearing her out of her recollections. "What was the pink cake you made the other day?"

"The *napolitains*?"

Another snap of long fingers with blood-red painted tips. "Exactly. Now that's unique. No one's ever made it before. Why is that?"

Shayne shrugged. "Because it is a Mauritian sweet, made and sold only in Mauritius."

Her grandmother had taught her how to make the little

cakes. Two biscuits of lightly cooked *pâte sablée* sandwiched together with a thin layer of jam and smothered over the top and sides with pink icing.

"Why can't you make more stuff like this? Unique stuff?"

"Because it's not what I trained to do. The recipes from Mauritius are for what my grandmother made while I went there. They don't exist in any cookbook. Every family has its own version and twist on the dishes."

"All the more reason for you to exploit them." Katya paused, to click away at her BlackBerry. She lifted those narrowed eyes onto Shayne again. "Speaking of unique, the network aired the pink cake recipe this morning during the Australian time slot. There's been a surge of viewers, and already hundreds of requests to put the segment up in the Videos section before the usual twenty-four-hour wait time."

Shayne's heartbeat accelerated. "That was a fluke. The *napolitains* recipe wasn't supposed to air before autumn."

"Fluke shmuke." Katya waved her free hand in the air. "The network wants more of the same kind of unique food, so I suggest you break your grandma's recipe logs and come up with something for us. We've got ten more shows to shoot based on the new premise."

On the bombshell, she left.

Shayne breathed out a sigh of relief, while Aurelie glanced at Katya's departing form with wide eyes.

"This will mean shooting every day for the next week at least. Are we ready for this?" Aurelie asked.

"Shoot what? I have no clue what else to offer her."

Panic gripped her throat in a stranglehold at the full extent of what rested upon her shoulders. Ten shows meant at least twenty recipes explained and carried out in minute detail. And Katya wanted her to make Mauritian food? She knew her basics, and her staples, thanks to having been forced to stay in the kitchen with her mother. But Mauritian food represented nothing distinctive, some dishes terribly rustic, even. Food influences were as wide and varied as Indian, Creole, and

Chinese. Very little original Mauritian food existed, at least, very little she could showcase on television. The food became as much a melting pot of origins as the cultures and religions were varied on the island.

What had she gotten herself into?

"Blast you, Grayson."

"What has he got to do with it?" Aurelie asked. "Wait, I know. You need some stress relief, and he's not here."

All thoughts of panic scorched to dust at the mortification that gripped her when she processed Aurelie's words. She sputtered and couldn't choke a word out.

"Come on, I saw him on the walk of shame back to his bedroom the morning he left. Who did you think you were kidding?"

Shayne opened her mouth and clamped it shut when words failed her.

"You miss him, admit it."

Yes, she did miss him. Especially because he no longer called. When he'd first gone to New York, he would call her every morning, at four. He'd find her in the kitchen, while his day started back on the East Coast. But his calls had dwindled, to stop altogether for the past four days.

He'd been gone for three weeks, and so far she'd refused to acknowledge whether theirs could've been nothing more than a fling to him.

Truth be told, Grayson had not promised her anything. He'd not even said if he'd be back, or when. He hadn't asked her to wait for him. Yes, he said he loved her, but how many men cried those three words in the throes of passion and forgot all about the significance of the statement the minute postcoital bliss sent them into deep sleep?

Aurelie placed a hand on hers and squeezed. "Call him."

How she wanted to, but how she dreaded the prospect. If he wanted to be in touch, he would've contacted her, wouldn't he?

The question remained with her throughout the afternoon. Pasting on a smile and finding out how much of a good actress she could be, she went ahead with the taping of the show. She did two basic recipes—Mauritian-style chicken curry with rice, and the island's summer drink, *alouda*, which she had to adapt because she didn't have *tukmaria*, the little black basil seeds that puffed up with a gel-like coating when soaked. With ice-cold milk, rose-flavored syrup, and shredded jelly, she swapped the missing ingredient with chia seeds and concocted something.

At eleven o'clock in the evening, she stared at the ceiling with eyes wide open. Despite being in Freewill for over a month, she still hadn't adapted to the time difference with London, and sleep refused to come when night hit Wyoming.

One a.m. in New York. What was Grayson up to?

She should call him.

Before she could lose the impetus, she grabbed her phone and dialed his number.

He answered on the third ring, with a curt, "Yes?"

"Hey," she mumbled. "It's me."

"Hi. Wait, let me move to the other room so I can hear you better."

His voice sounded weary, and tired. Distant, too? She gulped, and refused to contemplate this possibility. "How are you?"

She bit her lip before she could say *you didn't call.* She wasn't one of those clinging girlfriends, or those needy women who had to have a man to validate their existence.

"It's been one mess after the other. Clients fucking up, us having to pick the pieces, this goddamn market choosing now to play 'let's crash the Euro.'"

"You sound like you need a break."

Please say the only thing you need is me.

"I could do with one. Listen—"

"Gray?" a throaty voice definitely belonging to a woman sounded in the background.

Shayne's heart stopped. No, this couldn't mean—

"Come back. I need you," the woman said.

Shayne could hear the pout in the words, the possessive urgency. What could Grayson be doing at one a.m. with a sultry-toned woman who urged him to come back? To bed, surely?

"Robin, one minute," he said. His voice seemed to come from far away, as if he'd moved the phone from his mouth to say those words.

"I...I think you'd better go," Shayne blurted before her voice strangled.

She cut the call at the same time the first fat tear plopped onto the knuckle of her thumb, still poised on the End Call button.

No wonder he didn't call. He had someone else.

❧

Three days went by, during which she had no idea how she existed or got on with everything. She made food for the show, smiled, and laughed at the camera. Upon the arrival of Kristin Callahan, the new girls' team soccer coach, the townsfolk roped her in for the upcoming Fourth of July weekend two days away, and she let the effervescence carry her and blank her mind. Heck, she'd even had a Fourth of July special shoot, where she made American food with Aurelie and Tracy Parks' help. Seemed the audience had gone wild for that episode, aired just the previous day. The viewers loved the glimpse into personal life the show offered, into the personality of Shayne and Aurelie and how they interacted with those around them.

She'd fooled them all, putting on a happy face for the outside world to see. But try as might, the sultry, husky voice of the woman at Grayson's apartment refused to leave her memory. Every time she blinked, every second the chatter around her died, she heard the possessive tone sounding so convinced Grayson had better get back to her.

He hadn't called, either, which further confirmed he had washed his hands of her. Out of sight, out of mind. Did this happen to the poor Robin when Grayson came to Freewill?

Shayne snorted. Here she was feeling sorry for her rival. *Oh, get a grip on yourself!* Her *rival*? She'd never even been a contender in the race to have a relationship with Grayson

Warner. He'd had a tryst. Which she should've had, too, if she'd stuck to her usual MO.

What a daft idiot she'd turned out to be. No matter how much she'd sworn never to fall for a man, she'd gone and done just that. What could it be? Her guardrails not being in place once she left London? Back there, she knew who she was, what everyone expected of her, how she had to act to get on with the least possible ripple affecting the status quo in her life.

Then she'd left, to come here, where everything became a whole muck up of twisted shit that had hit the fan with no hope of her ever be able to clean the mess.

Shayne stopped on the threshold of the kitchen when she saw Katya prancing around focused on the screen of her BlackBerry. About to turn and head back upstairs to escape the barracuda, she wasn't fast enough. Katya looked up. And smiled.

Katya never smiled; the woman didn't have any range of emotion beyond "frown," and "frown some more."

"You are so not going to believe this."

Uh-oh. Trouble with a huge T.

"It appears your napolitana video—"

"*Napolitains*," Shayne corrected.

"Whatever. So it appears the video went viral and has attracted the attention of major food bloggers and journalists. Everyone wants to know who you are, and where you're from."

Panic welled up, to squeeze the air out of her chest all while it crushed her throat. This couldn't be happening. This is not what she had signed up for.

Really? What did you think you were getting into when you agreed to do a cooking show?

Bloody hell, she had jumped the gun. No way she could do it. It appeared she couldn't go back either. Or maybe she could?

"I quote," Katya started, "'combining the rustic authenticity of regular food like Anne Burrell with the very British sharp-mouthed slant of Gordon Ramsay, up-and-coming chef Shayne Morea softens this in-your-face approach and image with the food-porn sex appeal of Nigella Lawson and a touch of accessible hotness like that of culinary beauty queen Giada de Laurentiis. Her delightfully quirky cleaning routines are also a joy to watch. Where has she been hiding all this time?' Unquote."

Katya scrolled down on the phone. "'We've never seen a chef bring the islander touch to a cooking show. French-Guyana's Chef Babette has done it, but the English-speaking food channels did not have their unique slant. Until Shayne Morea came along. With parents hailing from the tiny island nation of Mauritius, the British hot babe shows how, in spreading her branches to as far as Freewill, Wyoming, she has not forgotten her roots to her ancestral land and culture.'"

Shayne gasped. They had to be kidding. Where on earth had she "honored her roots and ancestral ties"? Faced with a dilemma, dragon Katya breathing down her neck, she'd backed herself into a corner and had seen the way out as those decadent, crumbly and icing-covered cakes she'd loved ever since her first visit to Mauritius, when she was five.

Push came to shove, she wanted to scream. The world thought she embodied all that, when she proved nothing but a fraud.

"Good thing we snapped you up when we did." Katya gloated. "Thanks to those reviews, you are the rising star of the cooking world. It's why the network wishes to commission two more seasons of *Silly & Simple: Cooking with Shayne*."

"What?" The word came out as a croak, the question pinging into her brain like an out-of-control pinball zipping all over the place.

Katya bobbed her head up and down, which sent her blond mane flying every which way. How uncharacteristic of the usually composed producer. "Twenty-four shows, forty-five minutes each. Of course, we want Aurelie on there with you, but she might be busy with her game development, in which case we'd take you on and have a celebrity guest on a few shows."

Stop, she wanted to shout, but couldn't. "I can't do this."

"Of course you can. You've been doing great for the past few weeks, and nothing will change. We'll even keep shooting here in Freewill, if it's what you wish." She paused. "I don't think you really realize, Shayne. This show now takes place on your terms, with your conditions. Do you know how many would kill to be in your shoes? You didn't even have to slug through a reality-TV cooking competition to just get noticed. Bless your luck and count your blessings." The BlackBerry beeped. "I have to go," Katya said. "I expect an answer by tomorrow."

Shayne watched her breeze out of the kitchen. The cameraman and his grip boy were getting out of their van in the yard. A few barked orders from Katya and they clambered into the vehicle, to take a U-turn and return the irate woman to town.

Good riddance. She needed time to think, which she wouldn't be able to do with people around her. Katya's words rolled in her head in such a conflicting turmoil she felt sick to her stomach. Bile rose in her throat, and she reached the loo under the stairs just in time to chuck the bitter, acrid acid into the toilet bowl.

"Fuck! Are you okay?" Aurelie exclaimed behind her. "Oh my God! You're not pregnant, are you?"

What? She better not be. She and Grayson had taken their precautions, but what if...? No, just not possible.

Better not be possible. She had enough on her plate. Grayson had someone else. She'd been an exotic side dish, and he went back to his comfort fare of steak and potatoes. The bloody man could eat steak every day, a true cowboy.

Stop thinking of him. He left, remember?

Aurelie reached out and tugged Shayne's hair back into a ponytail. "What's the matter?"

Shayne straightened and washed her mouth out with water in the basin. After dabbing at her lips with the towel, she exited the loo and closed the door behind her. The worry in Aurelie's graphite-gray eyes and the scrunched skin of the narrow forehead shook her.

"The network just offered a contract for two more seasons."

"But that's wonderful. You made it."

Made it? Katya and Aurelie had to be kidding, right? If her mother found out about the show, she'd never live it down. A few videos on the Net weren't alarming, with her parents clueless about the Internet and anything on it. But a full-blown show and media coverage? She would never be able to go back to the life she'd left back in London.

And she couldn't stay in Freewill, where everywhere she looked, memories of her time with Grayson jumped to the fore.

Purgatory here, and Hell waiting on the other side of the pond. Where did it all leave her?

The breath crushed into her chest once again, her head going light. She snaked a hand out and braced her palm on the door frame. Her head spun, and she'd soon throw up again.

"Except that I don't want to have made it," she bit out. "I never wanted any of this. I came here to help you teach a sweet old lady how to make Indian sweets. Where did I sign up to become a celebrity chef?"

Aurelie planted her fists on her hips. "You're telling me you had no clue what you were getting into when you agreed to the show? Grow up, Shayne. You've been making choice after choice ever since you came over—"

"Oh, get out of here! I haven't—"

"You damn have, you snotty bitch."

Aurelie's eyes sparkled with anger. What had Shayne done to make the girl so mad?

"Choosing to leave London on a whim, ditching your mother's phone calls, moving on with the cooking lessons, making googly eyes at my cousin, taking on the show, falling in love with a man with whom you're having a summer affair. It's only now you wake up and realize you've stepped out of your comfort zone?"

Shayne took a step back, to bump into the closed door. Had she done all that? "I don't have a comfort zone, Aurelie."

"Yeah, right. When will you stop hiding your head in the sand? Admit it, you're scared shitless. It's what's got you in a tizzy."

The cheek of the girl.

"You've got to be kidding me. I'm not scared."

"Then why aren't you picking the damn phone and talking

to Grayson? You glance at that screen all day, but you never take the first step." She paused. "You know why? Because you're afraid of taking one step out of the safety boundaries you've set around you back in London and take a risk."

Incensed more because every word rang true when they hit home, Shayne responded by lashing out. "You're one to talk. What risk have *you* taken, you bloody cow?"

Aurelie poked a finger in Shayne's chest. "We're not talking about me here, but about you."

"How easy for you to sidestep the question."

"Not easier than you looking at all of it with woe-is-me goggles and refusing to face reality."

Aurelie turned and stalked out of the house, leaving Shayne fighting for breath in the hallway.

Blast be Aurelie. Shayne did not go all "woe-is-me," blaming the universe for what befell her. Everything since she'd stepped foot in Freewill had gone wrong, she could see it. Entirely her fault. What had happened to "live for the moment"? She'd forgotten her first rule here, and look where she landed. Mired in a mess, with a bright spotlight focused on her and a man she had fallen in love with returning to his real life and leaving her behind. After Pratik, she'd thought she'd learned her lesson, but she hadn't, bloody silly goat. She'd taken on more than she could chew here.

Freewill. Everything hinged on this. If she left, maybe she stood a chance that everything would fall back into place once again. Life in London will have changed, too, but London and Southall were her territories, her level playing ground. If she could find her balance, no matter how unstable it might turn out to be, in one place, that would be back home.

Home is where we want it to be.

Grayson's words flittered in, and she choked.

"Home isn't here for me," she said softly.

Because of this, she had to leave.

Fingers of cold and stinging dread closed around her heart when she reckoned leaving meant closure, and good-bye would seal the rift that had pushed her into this world, this alternate reality appearing like Heaven on Earth for a time.

She owed Grayson a farewell, an explanation, if only to wish him well with the rest of his life. *Closure. Always strive for closure*, her grandmother had told her. Funny how she remembered the words of *Nani Ma*, as she'd called her. Recalling her maternal grandmother's recipes brought forth memories of the old woman she'd thought long buried and forgotten.

Shayne wouldn't bear to hear Grayson's voice again. She'd break down, and beg him to give them another chance. She loved the bloody arsehole, for goodness' sake. No, she couldn't get in touch, not in a personal way. Something like a letter, or an e-mail, would do the job.

She blew out an exasperated sigh. She didn't even have his e-mail address. Maybe she could find it online, a contact address for his firm in New York.

She trudged upstairs to her room, where she had left the laptop yesterday after the Skype call to her mother. Once on the browser, she Googled Grayson's name and checked the results that came up.

The URL for his firm—*Warner, Elliott, & Gallas*—popped up first, followed by a few image results for him. Her gaze traveled to one of these pictures, a thumbnail of Grayson with his arm around a blonde.

No, it couldn't be.... Tears blurred her vision. He'd been taken all along? How had she allowed herself to fall for a man without knowing anything about him? She only chose to see what he showed here, but who on the ranch even knew him any longer? He'd been gone for fourteen bloody long years.

She should close the browser and forget about him. Obliterate him from her heart, and her mind. Force her body to drown out forever the all-encompassing feeling of absolution and completion that took over her whenever she lay in his arms.

But she was just a woman desperately in love, and she saw herself move the cursor onto the picture, clicking on it to be taken to the article where the image lay embedded.

The tears flowed when she skimmed the page. A few snippets stood out—"...one of New York's hottest bachelors now taken?..."; "...Robin Gallas being his plus-one at a few venues..."; "...more than meets the eye..."; "...sighted together over NYC since she broke up with high-powered playboy Chad Benedict...."

Shayne didn't need to read any more. She could simply stare at the picture and know in her heart she never stood a chance. Robin Gallas—the *Gallas* in his firm's name?—resembled a poised and sophisticated clone of the late Princess Diana, from the short, highlighted blonde hair to the sparkling blue eyes. Her smile appeared mysterious, as if privy to a secret, while she gazed fondly at Grayson, who had his arm draped around her waist. No one could mistake the adoration between them.

Effing idiot pathetic cow. Why hadn't she seen this picture before she gave her heart to that rat?

Closure, girl. You're looking for closure.

Biting her lip hard, she exited the window and returned to the search results page, where she clicked on the link for Grayson's firm and headed straight to the Contact Us page.

Copying Grayson's address and pasting it into the To box of her Hotmail message, she started typing.

> *Dear Grayson,*
> *Just wanted to let you know I am leaving Freewill shortly. It's been a delight to get to know you, and I'll cherish the moments we spent together. Thanks to you, I am no longer afraid of getting on a horse. :)*
> *All the best with your life back in New York.*
> *Fondly,*
> *S*

Chapter Ten

What the fuck—

Grayson stared at the e-mail. What did she mean by that? Shayne was supposed to stay in Freewill for the rest of the summer. Why would she leave so soon?

He glanced at his computer screen, the paired numbers of Forex exchange rates merging into a blur. *Focus.* He had to work his way out of this mess here before he could give his whole attention to Shayne's bombshell.

Try as he wished, he couldn't concentrate, and he ended up walking into Jay's office. Standing behind the executive chair, he reached across to the mouse and clicked the button to make the same report he'd been staring at appear on Jay's screen.

"You're still working on the Patterson account?" his friend asked. "You know it's a lost cause, right? No chance in hell we can recover the money that dick of Justin flambéed when we weren't looking."

"I promised Maeve Patterson I'd do my best to clear his shit. She's one of our oldest and most faithful clients. I couldn't let her down when she pleaded with me in the office the other day."

"Too bad the genes giving a good head on one's shoulders skipped her son's DNA."

"Tell me about it. But anyway, I've been working on this portfolio for the past week, and I think I see a pattern in the exchange rate on the Sydney market." He pointed at the highlighted numbers. "See there? We might be able to recoup much of her lost money if we manage to swoop in just before the market closes there. We have to do it today, though."

Jay turned to him. "Why are you telling me all this? I thought you were on the case exclusively."

"Because you're the one who will make the coup. I need to leave for Freewill ASAP."

"Trouble?"

"You don't know the half of it." *And neither do I.* He needed to speak to Shayne, stat, and find out what the hell was up with her. Her e-mail—a damn impersonal e-mail—had read cold and detached. Never would anyone suspect there'd been anything but a fleeting acquaintance between them. How could she do this to them? And more important, why?

He took a step away from the desk. "This is what it'll be like from here on, Jay. I'll be in Freewill, still working the market and trends over the Internet, while you and Robin will be responsible for the day-to-day running of the firm, managing the clients, and making the deals." He paused. "Our first test starts with the Patterson account."

Jay nodded. "We'll make it work."

"Good."

One less worry over his head. He could focus on Shayne and whatever the hell she thought of doing to them.

He speed dialed her number on his BlackBerry on the way back to his office. The call diverted to voice mail. No way would he leave a distanced message. He had to talk to her, if not in person, then at least over the phone.

At his desk, he didn't bother to shrug into his jacket. He pulled the garment over his arm while he tried to call her again. The damn voice mail once more. A sliver of unease darted in his gut. Was she avoiding him?

Aurelie would know. He dialed his cousin's number and bit back his impatience when she failed to answer after ten rings. Grayson called again. Maybe she was in the basement and didn't hear him.

As he emerged on the pavement, she answered as he managed to flag a cab. He slid into the car, muttered, "Upper East Side," to the cabbie before he greeted his cousin.

"What the hell is going on over there?" he asked.

"What do you mean?"

"Shayne is leaving."

"What?"

He winced at the screech. "She just sent me a three-line e-mail saying she was leaving Freewill shortly."

"And you're going to let her leave?"

Not the question he'd been expecting. "I have no intention of letting that happen."

"Good, because for a second there I thought you were gonna act like a stupid fool."

"Wait a second. What are you talking about? And what the hell is going on?"

"You really don't know? Why don't you call her and ask?"

"She's not picking up."

"Damn."

The way she said the word, the dejection in the tone, alarmed him. "Tell me what happened."

"The network's offered her a contract for two more seasons, and she's panicking because of it."

"But this doesn't mean she has to leave right away." *And why she wrote us off.*

"Grayson, you really have no idea, do you? She isn't panicking because of the show. She's just realized who she is, who she's been all this time, and the reality is too much for her."

What?

"And to top it all, she didn't have you when she most needed you," Aurelie finished.

"I was smoothing everything out so I could come back to her. What do you think I was doing?"

"Too late. She's under no illusions anymore."

Not if he could help it. "I'm coming back to Freewill on the first flight I can book."

He heard a snort and glanced up at the cab driver frowning at him in the rearview mirror.

"Good luck finding a place on a flight out, son. You forgot it's the Fourth of July weekend?"

Damn. He *had* forgotten. He could be stuck for days trying to get a seat.

Unless he did this the hard way. He nodded at the cabbie and returned to the call. "I'm driving over. You have to promise me to do everything you can to keep Shayne in Freewill until I get there."

"Everything?"

God, how he hated the way his cousin seemed to perk up at the mention of his carte blanche. He had no other choice, though.

"Everything," he confirmed.

Shayne was worth all the trouble Aurelie could get him in.

෨

Saturday dawned bright and sunny. On her daily walk to catch the morning humidity, Shayne witnessed the sun break over the horizon. Two thin, flat lines of light spreading north and south from a distinct point east, that were gone in a blink when the brightness swallowed the dark of night away.

The day promised to be hot and dry. Perfect for the mayor's garden party to kick off the Fourth of July celebrations. On the actual fourth, there would be the Firemen's Dance and the fireworks display.

She'd wanted to be out of here already. If it were up to her, she'd have been back in London. But out of the blue, Pavel, the cameraman, had blurted in front of a furious Katya how he'd mistakenly deleted the last two days' worth of shooting, and he'd forgotten to do a backup. Shayne thus found herself stuck here to shoot those recipes again. After this debacle, both Mrs. Harvey and Tracy Parks cornered her into staying for the celebrations, while Lynn Gilmore urged her to show Kristin Callahan the ropes in training the girls' team.

Maybe the hype and revelry would help keep her mind away from the thought of Grayson. She'd crossed paths with both Mika and Jed during the past mornings, both men raising a quirked eyebrow when she declined the offer to take Bella out on a walk, as she'd done every day after Grayson had left. Her heart no longer found itself in the act, in the joy Grayson had awakened in her to ride along the plains and lose her breath every time at the stark beauty of the Wyoming landscape. She'd hated the place when she first came here, but she'd grown to love the wilderness so much that she yearned for this land today. It would kill her to leave. Freewill had started to feel like home, because her heart rested here, with a man who had won her over, and left....

Stop it. She picked up her pace to reach the back porch.

Her cell phone vibrated in her jeans pocket, the blare of bhangra drums slicing through the early morning quiet in a jarring manner.

Her breath quickened as she reached for the device. Would it be Grayson? He'd called the day before. Twice. Then, nothing. *Just as well.* She sighed at the sight of Dave's number on the screen.

"Hey," she mumbled in greeting.

"Before you start cursing me, please know I did nothing and never sold you out."

"What are you talking about?"

"Dad's on the other line. He wants to talk to you."

"No, wait—" She stopped at the beep signaling he'd connected the three of them over a conference call. "Dad?"

Her heart hammered, blood pounding in a *whoosh* against her temples. Her father, though she was certain he loved her, never spoke to her unless to urge her to make something out of her life.

"Hey, Shayne," he answered. "We need to talk."

She gulped at his clipped tone. She couldn't remember her

father ever laughing, or seeming relaxed. He portrayed the stereotype of the staid and straitlaced accountant down to the last cliché.

"I...I'm coming back. Right after the weekend, actually," she blurted.

"What will I do with you? Get on Skype; I just sent you a connect request. You and I need to have a serious talk."

"Skype? You're on Skype?"

"I'm cutting the call. I expect you online within the next two minutes."

The click on the line told her he'd disconnected. The call still went on, though. Dave.

"Did he just tell me to get on Skype, or did I dream it up?" she asked her brother.

"He did, and I suggest you get your arse in gear 'cause he did sound like he meant what he said."

She shouldn't keep him waiting. A form of daughterly duty automatic control took over, smothering the haze of disbelief at the thought that her father not only knew what the Internet was but also had an account on Skype. Where else could he be? Facebook? Did he read her tweets? And if he could log onto the Net, he must've seen the videos and the shows, read the many reviews and articles. Her whole life seemed to be splashed online these past few weeks—had he seen it all, too?

Dread weighted her feet when she climbed upstairs and reached her bedroom. She flopped onto the bed and pulled the laptop onto the mattress. Indeed, when she flipped the screen open and accessed Skype, the connect request from Girish Morea sat right there on the program's home screen. The tiny icon next to his name blinked green, which meant he was online.

Shayne tapped her finger on the mouse pad to accept the request and start a video call.

A square screen popped up, black, before the image cleared and her father stared at her. His thin hair buzzed short, face lean and smooth, with the rimless glasses sitting on his beaky nose—the nose she'd inherited, albeit in a less beaky form—he seemed every inch the chartered accountant.

"You look a fright," he said.

She'd just been out in the wind, her loose hair in a thick tangle around her face. She scooped the locks up and tied them into a bun with an elastic band.

"How are you, Dad?"

He pursed his lips. "Question is, how are *you*?"

She shrugged, forced a weak smile. "Good."

"I would think the woman who just started an absolute tizzy inside the BBC ranks would be feeling more than good."

Did she hear humor in his tone? And what the hell was he talking about? "I beg your pardon?"

He shrugged, the movement so eerily like hers and Dave's. "The BBC Two and Channel Four journalists have been having a fit for the past week. They're saying, 'If Shayne is British, why did the Americans discover her? And why isn't she doing a show for us, instead of WGN?'"

Was that a smile on his face? "I don't think I'm following you here."

"They would've been more peeved if the French had offered you the show; Americans are the lesser evil."

"You know about the show?"

"I'm not exactly fond of the fact that you've kicked Nigella off the culinary porn queen throne—"

She choked, and brought a hand up to her mouth.

"—but you've done good for yourself. Your very own cooking show? Well done."

"But," she started, and stopped, at a loss for words.

"But what?" he asked gently.

His voice reminded her of the way he would murmur sweet words and sing Bollywood oldies to her when she was little. How had she forgotten about those moments?

With a cramp along her heart, she reckoned the memory of him telling her she belonged in a kitchen and nowhere else had obliterated everything ever since she turned into a teen, when her mother had started to steer her toward being the "proper" daughter-in-law for her upcoming nuptials to a suitable boy.

"You want to see me settled, remember? Settled and married and being a good daughter-in-law. Celebrity does not fit in there, does it?"

She couldn't keep the bitterness out of her voice. He must've heard, because he flinched.

"When did I ever say this?"

Let the masks fall; let's have it all out in the open. Aurelie was right. She'd walked on eggshells back in London and refused to do anything that could send a ripple into her carefully constructed environment.

But not anymore. In for a penny, in for a pound.

And stop with the stupid idioms.

"Come on, Dad. For as long as I can remember, you've told me my place was in the kitchen, with Mum. That when the time came, you expected me to do the right thing."

"Which you did."

The quiet certainty in his words, as well as the small smile on his face, jolted her.

"Do you remember when I started telling you you belonged in a kitchen?"

She shook her head.

"Right after I'd tasted your very first try at making *aloo gobi*."

"I was nine, with no clue what I was doing. I just threw the potatoes with the cauliflower and let it cook."

"You never noticed how I always asked *you* to make the dish afterward?"

He *had* requested that.... She'd always thought he wanted her to perfect her cooking skills, because she "belonged in a kitchen."

"And why do you think I didn't bat an eye when you asked me to fund your courses at Le Cordon Bleu in London, even when you decided to do a stint at their Paris institute? And your *Chak Le India* tour to learn about every type of Indian cuisine?"

Too much, too fast. Her head reeled, and she couldn't make sense of his words. "Let me get this straight. What exactly are you telling me?"

"That I knew ever since you were nine you belonged in a kitchen, Shayne. That's what you did best, effortlessly."

No, he couldn't mean it....

"You've got your grandmother's touch." He chuckled. "Thank God you never became a shrew like her, but no one could rival my mother-in-law's cooking. No one but you."

So, all along, she'd misunderstood him? "What about settling down?"

"With those daft idiots your aunts paraded before you? Or that dog of Pratik? None of these men is good enough for my little girl."

Did he blush when he said those words?

Her heart swelled, and tears stung her eyes, to roll down her cheeks. "Daddy, I didn't know."

Her voice sounded low, hoarse. With one hand, she reached out and touched the screen, imagined she ran the tip of her fingers against his cheek, instead of the outline of his face from the camera.

She used to touch him thus, as a little girl. Every night, he'd put her to bed, and she'd insist he be the one to tuck her in, not her mother. With a startled gasp, she recalled the first time he'd gone away on a business trip. She must've been three, and the tantrums she'd thrown onto her mother during his absence were epic.

Then they'd grown further and further apart, the older she got. She'd thought him condescending and tyrannical, sexist and old-fashioned. While all along, he'd seen her already for who she was and simply steered her onto the path she should take.

"I'm sorry."

When he smiled at her, the chasm between them crumbled onto itself.

"I remembered the taste of your *napolitains* when I watched the show the other day. When will you make some for me?"

Through her tears, she grinned. "The minute I come back."

The elation of bridging the gap with her father crashed when she realized she'd be in London soon. Freewill would be behind her, with Grayson on another continent.

Grayson with Robin. She forced the flare of jealousy and the pang of loss to smother out from her heart.

"I just wanted you to know I'm proud of you."

Her throat clogged even more.

"Daddy, I have to go," she mumbled.

She wasn't fit to think of Grayson in her state, and the last thing she wanted was for her father to see her crumbling because of a man. She'd also crave to tell him how the Grayson Warner she had known here in Freewill embodied everything she'd ever wanted, and he'd have been worthy of Girish Morea's little girl.

But she couldn't.

"Take care of yourself, *beti*."

The Indian endearment for beloved daughter.

"Will do, Daddy," she croaked out, before she cut the call and slammed the laptop closed.

Shayne didn't know how long she remained in the room. The tears coursed down her face, to stop at some point, because when she blinked back to reality, the moisture had dried into salty trails on her skin. Her eyes felt gritty, and they burned. In her mouth, she had the bitter taste always accompanying crying.

The unexpected conversation with her father had put everything into perspective. She hadn't been pushed to become a chef; she'd wanted to all along but never realized it. The reason she'd excelled at the culinary institute, why she'd picked up every nuance from every regional cuisine in India, despite the language barrier with most of the inhabitants. Also why she'd enjoyed teaching Mrs. Harvey and her crew how to make the sweets, and why, on some days, she'd felt so at ease in front of the camera. Not because she could be a good actress, but because she was a chef, and a bloody good one at that.

Grayson had been right.

She stifled the sob threatening to pour out.

Ever since the day they met, Grayson had seen right through her, into her heart. He'd known who she was, Lord knew how. The press and business articles all said he had the Midas touch, everything he handled turned to gold.

He'd touched her life and made her become whole. With him, she'd come into her own. In Freewill, she'd discovered her real self, and answered her true calling. All of which had allowed her to be who she was meant to be: a celebrity chef. Someone who enjoyed teaching and sharing her passion about food with others. She'd never felt more at ease, more at home, on the show's set than on the days when she made her grandmother's recipes and recounted a bit of her childhood with the imagined audience.

Katya was right. She held something here, and she'd be a fool to let all of it go.

Shayne stood. She'd do the show. But not from here. Staying at Heart's Anchor would be too painful. Grayson's touch had brightened her world and opened new perspectives, but it had also battered her heart and left it dying with the pain of loss.

How can you lose what was never yours, Shayne?

She had to focus on what she had.

Slowly, she went down the stairs, to find Aurelie and inform the girl of her decision.

"I'm going to do the show, but not from here. I'm going back to London, and WGN has a studio there. Katya told me you've already bowed out of the next seasons because you're busy with the new game."

"You're leaving? But you can't do that. You have to stay here."

"I...." She faltered. She better come clean with her best friend. "I can't stand to be here and think of him every time I turn a corner."

"But Grayson loves you, and he's going to come back."

She shook her head. "I thought he loved me, but I was wrong. And if, when, he comes back, he won't be alone."

"What do you mean?" Aurelie's eyes had narrowed.

"He's got someone else in New York."

"Get out of here! He wouldn't—" Aurelie frown grew fierce. "The rat! You better tell me everything."

ೞ

Grayson hadn't wanted to stop. But right after he crossed the New York state border, a freak storm had hit and forced him to seek refuge at a dilapidated diner on Route 66. The drive to Freewill would already have taken a good number of hours notwithstanding this forced stop. The cabbie had been right; he'd failed to find a single seat on any plane going to Wyoming this weekend. His Porsche Cayman could eat the miles in a blink, if only the damn weather cooperated.

His BlackBerry rang. He pulled it out to find Aurelie's picture on the screen.

He didn't have time to bring the phone to his ear before her curse split his hearing.

"You fucking swine! How could you do this to her, you conniving, two-timing jerk?"

"What are you talking about?"

"How could you sleep with Shayne and profess to love her when you've got someone else waiting for you back in New York? I never expected this from you, of all people."

He'd been reaching for his cup of coffee when she slung the accusation. The jolt of surprise that zinged through him made him topple the mug. The scalding-hot liquid raced down the table to splash onto his lap before he could move out of the booth.

"Fuck!" he cursed.

"Exactly, you pig."

The waitress came over, appearing too eager to blot the coffee from his stained pants. He grabbed the wad of tissues in her hand and moved out of her range.

"What the heck is going on, Aurie? Why are you accusing me of something I haven't done?"

She snorted. "Shayne heard her."

"Her who?" Would the woman make sense, finally?

"Robin." His cousin spat the name out.

"What has Robin got to do with this?"

"So you don't deny she exists? The gall of you, you.... I don't even have a curse word strong enough for the likes of you!"

"Aurelie, Robin is my business partner—"

She snorted again.

"—and no less a sister to me than you are."

"Then why was she urging you to come back into her bed?"

He choked on his saliva. "What?"

"Shayne heard her, one night when she phoned you. Robin called you back the minute you started speaking to Shayne."

He forced his mind to remember the call. *Wait a second.* That had been on the night the Euro took the plunge. "We were monitoring the market. Robin was panicking because she doesn't have the kind of coolheaded guts to swoop in and play the market in last-minute deals like Jay and I do. We were on the verge of closing a deal, hence why she needed me."

He closed his eyes. Everything made sense; Shayne had jumped to conclusions. She was leaving because she thought he had someone else. Not because she didn't love him.

"You swear?" Aurelie asked in a small, deflated voice.

"On my mother's grave."

The solemnity must not have escaped her. He didn't kid with the notion of his mother, or her death.

"Okay," she muttered. "What do we do now?"

He had to get to Freewill as quickly as possible, freak storm or not. "You've made sure she has to stay in town for the weekend?"

"Yes. I got the show's crew to rope her in for a couple more shootings, for a price—"

He cringed at those words, and refused to imagine what the

cost could be.

"—and Mrs. Harvey, Mom, and Lynn are keeping her busy with the celebration plans." She paused. "Shayne really is leaving, Grayson. She's agreed to do the show, but from London. We don't have much time here."

Damn. All the more reason for him to get back right away.

"Just keep her there until I get back. I'm coming as quickly as I can."

CƷ

He reached Freewill just past midday. The sun blazed strong and high in the Wyoming sky, beating down his back and searing through the thin cotton shirt he'd worn under his suit. The jacket lay discarded on the passenger seat, and he dismissed the garment as easily as he blanked the incessant beeping from the car. He'd pushed the Porsche to its limit on the drive, the tank almost empty because he'd refused to stop to refuel a third time. Who cared? He needed to get back, and here he was.

He had to go find Shayne, but he had something else he needed to do. No new beginning, no clean future for him until he took that last step to put his past behind him.

Grayson flew into the house to take the stairs three by three to reach his bedroom. He ditched his loafers, the coffee-stained linen pants, and the still-damp boxers underneath, to slide, commando, into a pair of jeans. The shirt came off in a dumped ball, and he pulled a white T-shirt over his torso.

All the way back out of the house, stopping in the mudroom off the kitchen to toe on his riding boots, and pluck the cowboy hat from the peg. His brain would scramble under the scorching sun without the protection.

On a quick jog, he reached the empty stables, everyone being downtown at the mayor's garden party to kick off the Fourth's celebrations. Just as well he found himself alone; he didn't have time for chitchat or even greetings. He saddled

Black Beauty and climbed onto the stallion's back. The big beast seemed as impatient as him, and Grayson let it have free rein to gallop across the plains, on the way to the hills.

He slowed the pace when he reached the rambling slopes. A force tugged him back when he set out to embark on the left trail to the hilltop, and the horse pranced with nervous energy.

He could do it. He had to.

On a deep breath, he steered the horse up the hill.

The last time he'd made the climb had been on foot, following his parents' caskets on the day of their funeral. There'd been exceptional rain that August, on the eve of the fateful day, so the slopes had been wet and slippery. The grass had been as brown as the mud caking the landscape.

Today, the path ambled up the climb dry and rocky. Green grass surrounded the edges, dotted here and there with colorful wild flowers. Birds chirped in the air, and butterflies flitted around.

He made the stallion still when he reached the top. The two tombstones, side by side, sat there on the evened-out hilltop. When he'd left them, they'd been heaps of muddy earth.

Grayson dismounted. Tugging the bridle in his hand, he made the animal move forward along with him. No tree around to tie the reins, so he had to keep them in his grip to prevent the horse from running off. Good thing, because the soft leather in his hands gave him something to hold on to. He needed the contact, in a lifeline holding him firmly on this side of existence, not on the other side where his parents and all their pain and suffering lay.

He removed his hat when he stopped a few feet from the graves. His eyes trained on the tombstone of his mother's final resting place, he wanted to open his mouth and talk to her. But words eluded him, and he settled for silence. She would understand, for in his silence lay his respect and his love for her.

She was at rest, finally.

And so was his father.

With reluctance, he tore his gaze from one tombstone to

gaze at the other. Robert Jefferson Warner. The man who'd never deserved the title of beloved father or loving husband.

The knowledge sliced through him hard, to clutch at his guts. His father might've been a total fuckup, but he'd loved his wife.

Today, Grayson knew the pain of thinking you'd lost the woman you loved. All through this trip, he'd asked himself how he would live without Shayne, without the woman who made the whole difference in his world. In his mind, he'd heard the echo of the same desperation in his father's voice when Bobby Warner had begged Grayson to tell him how he was supposed to go on.

His father had loved his mother. In a twisted, messed-up way, but he'd loved her nevertheless.

A shot of redemption for his father's soul coursed through him, and upon the realization, Grayson blinked. A soft breeze blew around him, enveloped him in a hug. He could almost believe the embrace felt like his mother's, on those odd moments when she had bestowed her genuine love on him.

"I've met her," he told his mother, staring at her grave. "The princess you said I would find under the arch of the rainbow."

He grinned, feeling equally stupid for talking to her this way and for believing he earned her blessing the minute the words left his mouth.

"I'm going to bring her home, Mom. I promise."

He turned to the horse, and climbed back into the saddle.

Time is running out.

While the horse galloped down the hillside and across the plains, he reached the ranch. One glance at his Porsche and he knew the vehicle wouldn't take him into town. He'd also be hard pressed to find a car with everyone at the festivities.

Black Beauty whinnied and stomped the ground with a hoof.

"I know I have you, old boy," he told the stallion. "Let's go find Shayne."

CB

Why did everyone whisper when their eyes alighted on her? Shayne tried hard to brush off the odd glances sent her way as she waded around the town. The many stalls selling candy floss and other fair-type food failed to catch her attention, and she squirmed under yet another stare burning into her back.

What was it with the people? No one had acted star-struck on her previous trips to town, and today, they treated her like a snobby celeb?

She concealed a grimace when she glimpsed Aurelie stalking in her direction. She tried to nip into a side lane, but she wasn't quick enough. Aurelie caught up and grabbed her arm in a vise-like hold.

"Look over there. The handsome sheriff and his even hotter deputy, with Officer Pandoah. I swear to you, their uniforms are so tight you can make out the ridges of their six-pack abs under the shirts. Shall we go see?"

She tried to shrug her friend off. "I have no desire to see their abs, or anyone else's. What is wrong with you today? You've been pulling me this way and that ever since the morning."

A hush fell over the crowd. All eyes turned toward Main Street, before they returned to her, and back onto the road again. What the hell—

Shayne spun around and stood frozen at the sight greeting her. A tall, handsome cowboy galloped on a mighty black beast. The hat hid his face, but she could swear it was Grayson.

No, it couldn't be....

Even from the rapid gallop, he stopped the horse in a graceful move and descended from the animal.

Aurelie's mother ran to him, and he tipped his hat back to exchange a few words with her while he clutched something she passed into his grip.

The breath whooshed out of Shayne. Indeed, the man who'd come galloping into town proved none other than Grayson

Warner.

What was he doing here?

Out of the corner of her eye, she saw Pavel, her cameraman from WGN, steer his camera in Grayson's direction.

"Warner, what do you think you're doing? Main Street is off-limits for horses," the sheriff bellowed.

Shayne glanced at the handsome Native American man. He'd taken a few steps in their direction, but then a beautiful blonde woman grabbed his arm, pulled him back, and whispered something in his ear. The sheriff scowled. He then glanced at Grayson and tipped his hat.

What on earth went on here?

Shayne turned back toward Grayson, to gasp when she found his sinful, T-shirt-clad chest barely a foot from her.

He reached into his pocket for his phone. She could barely move while he speed dialed a number and handed her the cell.

"There's someone you should talk to," he said, in the smooth, lazy drawl she had so missed. No matter how much she replayed their conversations in her mind, the memories could never compare to the actual sound of his voice.

He still held the phone. Shayne glanced left and right, to find everyone watching them. With thick fingers, she reached for the BlackBerry, making sure her hand didn't touch Grayson's, and brought it to her ear.

"Hello?" she said.

"Shayne, it's Robin Gallas."

The gravelly voice sounded less husky, but no mistaking the same tone she had overheard when she'd called Grayson. Everything inside her turned to solid ice. A lick of frostbite danced down her spine, burning the skin to a raw, open wound.

"So Grayson tells me you believe he and I are together." Robin laughed. "So totally eek, girl. That'd be like a thing with my brother or something. Totally icky. I love him to bits, as he does me, but we're the siblings neither of us had. Nothing else."

"But—"

"He's in love with you, Shayne. In all the years I've known

Gray, he's never been so worked up over a girl as he's been over you. Makes me long to meet you as soon as possible so I can find out who got the upper hand on this guy." Robin spoke even faster than Aurelie. She laughed again. "You take care, all right? And don't torture him. Well, not too much."

Robin cut the call. The sultry voice still echoing in her head, a bemused Shayne returned the BlackBerry to Grayson.

So if Robin wasn't with Grayson, and if he loved her, Shayne, this meant....

Grayson smiled. He placed a hand on her shoulder, and made her turn slightly, where he pointed toward a beautiful woman with a long, black braid. "Billie Jensen," he said. "Scandinavian and Shoshone origins."

One by one, he pointed at people in the townsfolk of Freewill.

"Officer Treynor Pandoah, Shoshone. Jed Gilmore, Scottish and Native American. Lynn Miller-Gilmore, Irish, Scottish, and Scandinavian. Sheriff Hawk Blackwater, Caucasian and Yavapai. Aurelie Parks, African American, Cajun, and French."

Then he faced her.

"Grayson Warner. Scottish, with a Japanese great-grandmother somewhere along the way, as well as a Native American or two and an African American ancestor."

He grew silent.

Shayne parted her lips when his chocolate-brown eyes with the slanted corners focused on her. What did he wish to say? And could he just bloody say it already?

"For all of us, Freewill, Wyoming, is home." He paused. "You hail from London, with throwbacks to Mauritius and India. That's not any different or quirkier origins than most of us here."

Her tongue unglued from her roof of her mouth. "What are you trying to say?"

In the silence surrounding them, they'd hear if a pin dropped. Everyone, including her, seemed to hold their breaths.

"Freewill is home to all of us because we wished it to be our home." He drew a step closer to her. "I left here fourteen years ago, yet when I came back, I knew here is where I wanted to be. This is my home."

He released her shoulders, and as if in slow motion, he lowered his big frame in front of her.

"This is the home I want to make, the place where I want to bring my children up. But nothing of all that is ever going to happen if I don't have you."

He got down on his knees. Shayne gasped and brought a hand up to cover her mouth and stifle the sound.

"Give it a chance. Give us a try. Me, Heart's Anchor, Freewill."

He reached into his pocket, and when he pulled out the ring, all the women in the surroundings gave a collective gasp. Shayne didn't gasp, though, because her heart had stopped beating. Her lungs hurt, and whatever he said swam in her head.

But somehow, she heard the next words.

"Shayne Morea, will you do me the honor of becoming my wife?"

Sunlight glinted off the clustered diamonds in the platinum setting. But Shayne didn't glance at the ring. Instead, she stared into Grayson's eyes, plundered those dark depths to find their innermost secret. Yet all she saw was love, desire, and need.

An echo of her own feelings for him.

He'd come back.

The first tear slid down her cheek, followed by a veritable river punctuated by a sob, half a laugh, and half a sigh of relief.

Grayson frowned, and Shayne smiled through the tears. She better put him out of his misery.

"Yes," was all she said.

Epilogue

Shayne stifled a smile as she perused the transfixed expression on her face when Grayson had proposed. Did all women receiving the proposal seem so beatifically dumb?

Three weeks from the fateful day, and WGN aired the proposal scene that day at the end of a cooking segment.

At first, she'd wondered why Pavel had taped the scene, to later find out how Aurelie had wrangled with Katya and the crew to get them to keep her in Freewill for the weekend to give Grayson a chance to propose. Katya, seeing a scoop, had bargained for the exclusive right to get the scene on tape and air it during the show.

It appeared everyone in Freewill had known Grayson was on his way back to propose and they had to keep her in town. Seemed like the townsfolk were as meddling as Aurelie.

The diamond ring on her finger felt heavy. She lifted her hand, to stare once again at the timeless beauty of the jewel. Grayson's mother's engagement ring, what Aurelie's mum had slipped into his grip that day.

Shayne stood from the kitchen table and left the laptop behind. She walked to the sink, where, across the window, she could make out the silhouettes of the ranch hands and Grayson coming back from a horseback trip around the property to check on the fences. Summer in full force, they'd started to move the cattle from field to field, thus the need for secure fences.

Slowly but surely, she was turning into a cowgirl. She giggled. Who'd have thought, over two months ago, she'd be here today, thousands of miles from the only home she had known, and engaged to a man she loved with all she had and who adored her even more?

All thanks to her best friend's deceitful ruse to bring her here. She could never thank Aurelie enough.

Shayne frowned when a very distraught Aurelie rushed into the kitchen and plopped down onto a chair. She searched for the smartphone with a glance, because Aurelie didn't go anywhere without her phone, which seemed grafted to her hand. None around, and the flimsy sundress didn't look as if it held pockets to conceal the device.

"What's the matter?"

"You'll think I'm crazy if I tell you."

You're already off your rocker, girl. She didn't say it, though. "Try me."

Aurelie shivered, and she brought her hands up to rub along the goose-bumped flesh of her naked arms.

Shayne's concern grew the more the girl remained silent. "What's wrong?"

Aurelie's lower lip trembled. "You know how the idea of *Vanorra: Blades of Mythos* came to me in a dream, right? I've dreamed of her so many times, seeing her world and imagining the rest of her life."

"Yeah. So?"

Aurelie glimpsed over her shoulder, as if something—or someone—stood there. "I was writing an algorithm downstairs when I suddenly fell asleep. And I dreamed of her." She paused. "Except, this time, I *became* her. Vanorra. I saw everything through her eyes, and then this man appeared. Something inside me knew his name was Bren."

"Well, that's spooky, but it was just a dream, innit?"

"I'm not sure."

"Why do you say this?"

"Because when I woke up, as abruptly as I'd fallen asleep, I still heard her voice, Shayne." Aurelie glanced up, eyes wide with terror. "She said, 'Bren is coming.'"

Shayne left the sink to go hug her friend. "It was just a dream."

A shard of unease danced in her body, because she could clearly recall the ghostly voice that had whispered in her ear a few times here. Could this same spirit be messing with Aurelie?

But then she shrugged the feeling off. If the ghost existed, she'd proved peaceful. Hadn't she brought Shayne and Grayson together that day at the creek?

"Tell you what. We need to start working on the wedding plans," she said to lighten the atmosphere.

Because everything started in Freewill and ended here. She'd found her happy ending here; why shouldn't Aurelie find hers?

~ABOUT THE AUTHOR~

Stories about love, life, relationships...in a melting-pot of culture.

Zee is an author who grew up on a fence - on one side there was modernity and the global world, on the other there was culture and traditions. Putting up with the culture for half of her life, one day she decided she'd stand tall on her wall and dip toes every now and then into both sides of her non-conventional upbringing.

From this resolution spanned a world of adaptation and learning to live on said wall. The realization also came that many other young women of the world were on their own fence.

This particular position became her favorite when she decided to pursue her lifelong dream of writing - her heroines all sit 'on a fence', whether cultural or societal, in today's world or in times past, and face dilemmas about life and love.

Hailing from the multicultural island of Mauritius, Zee is a degree holder in Communications Science. She is married, mum to a tween son, & stepmum to a teenage lad.

You can visit Zee at:
www.zeemonodee.blogspot.com

Winds of Change

To be with him feels like playing Russian roulette blindfolded all while knowing she bet from borrowed lease. Can something this wrong be....right?

Neha Hemant has always been called the neutral one—like sensible Switzerland. She's never rocked the boat, and has always done everything expected from her, an Indo-Mauritian woman.

So where's the fulfillment, the sense of completion...?

And worse, why does she find this feeling of coming home with a man totally not right for her? She's a widow with three teenage children, and Logan Warrington is a reformed bad boy, and her boss.... He shouldn't have the power to make her burn, make her yearn and wish for nothing more than damning the consequences, not when she has lived her whole life trying to do what society expected of her.

As the winds of change blow on Neha's life, could the time have come for her to step out of her bubble, and live for the moment, and herself?